'Cruise-crime . . . ingeniously has its murder
back in England. Like a cruise: leisurely,
comfortable and meal-dominated.' *The Times*

Elizabeth Lemarchand is a retired
schoolmistress and lives near Exeter. This is
her fifth detective novel.

Cyanide with Compliments

Elizabeth Lemarchand

Mayflower

Granada Publishing Limited
Published in 1973 by Mayflower Books Ltd
Frogmore, St Albans, Herts AL2 2NF

First published in Great Britain by
MacGibbon and Kee Ltd 1972
Copyright © Elizabeth Lemarchand 1972
Made and printed in Great Britain by
Richard Clay (The Chaucer Press) Ltd
Bungay, Suffolk
Set in Linotype Plantin

To Charlotte Dyer

ONE

It must be the light up here, and the utter remoteness, Olivia Strode thought. It's gone to my head. I feel absolutely on top of the world, metaphorically as well as literally . . .

The Moreton-Blakes had insisted on her having the window seat. They were flying out to Venice together on the first stage of a cruising holiday, and it was her first journey by air. She glanced round at them. Professor Charles Moreton-Blake was making short work of *The Times* crossword. Molly, his wife, was leaning back composedly with her eyes closed, spruce as usual with her curly silver hair and complexion pink and fresh as a girl's. Olivia reflected that air travel must be a commonplace to them. They had even flown to the States by the Polar route.

There was a slight vibration, and the pulsating roar of the engines changed almost imperceptibly. Far below the gleaming white knife-edges of the Alps had vanished and the descent to Venice had started. The air hostesses were passing swiftly up and down the gangway removing the last traces of lunch. People hitherto invisible began to reveal their presence behind the high backs of the seats. Olivia's qualms about the enforced intimacies of life on board a cruise ship suddenly returned in force.

Molly Moreton-Blake opened her eyes and sat up.

'We've started to lose height,' she said. 'Quick, Olivia, the loo, before there's a queue the length of the plane. Let us out first, Charles. Heavens,' she added as they struggled to their feet 'how they do jam you up on these charter flights.'

By the time they had manoeuvred themselves back into their places the ground plan of the Lombardy Plain had filled in. Now there was not merely a framework but activities going on within it. A thin brown and yellow caterpillar of a train lay apparently motionless along a straight railway track. Minute cars gyrated in endless succession at a big roundabout. Instead of uniform olive greenness there was a variegated pattern of cultivation. An untidy urban sprawl came into view, flinging out tentacles of growth. A sudden crackle from a loudspeaker broke in on Olivia's fascinated contemplation.

'Ladies and gentlemen,' announced a feminine voice with the perfunctory courtesy of a routine announcement, 'in a few minutes we shall be landing at Marco Polo airport, Venice. Please fasten your seat belts and extinguish all cigarettes. After the aircraft has touched down kindly remain seated until...'

Olivia wrestled with her safety belt. Then, at an exclamation from Molly Moreton-Blake, she glanced down quickly and saw Venice, a handful of jewels scattered on glass ... the great mass of the Salute, the sweep of the Grand Canal flanked by its palaces, the clustered domes of St Mark's white in the sunlight, campanili shooting skywards like arrows. How incredibly shallow the lagoon was, its film of water scored by the acute-angled washes of little boats ...

The transition from delight to nightmare was too swift to register. As horizontality and verticality suddenly ceased to have significance her heart gave a huge painful leap ... The lagoon was a wall of water. The Salute swept up and vanished like a leaf in a storm, and campanili were levelled gun barrels. It flashed through her mind that a crash was imminent, and this was a premonition of survival in a non-spatial context. Then the aircraft which had banked on coming in to land flattened out over the anticlimax of grass and runways. Olivia, simultaneously relieved, ashamed and amused at herself, was thankful to see that Molly Moreton-Blake was absorbed in the contents of her handbag and would have missed any obvious sign of panic.

Now the airfield was flowing past at a more decorous rate. There was a small impact, an abrupt slackening of speed and at last, a halt. Conversation and people burst out on all sides, and there was frantic groping for hand baggage in the overhead racks. Charles Moreton-Blake whisked down his party's coats.

'Rear door,' he said, leading the way.

It was odd how, in the moment of landing, the comforting security of the aircraft was metamorphosed into claustrophobic imprisonment. The wait to be released was almost unbearable. At last the doors were opened and the steps wheeled into position. A slow forward shuffle began, and Olivia emerged into Italian sunshine to be greeted by a vista of tarmac, petrol tankers and a control tower of sinister space-age aspect. Domes, campanili and shining water had vanished like a dream. Glancing behind her she saw the Trident as a huge elongated egg prolifically hatching humanity.

'Feeling let down?' asked Charles Moreton-Blake, as they

waited their turn at the passport control. 'It's preposterous arriving this way, of course. One needs the sea approach to be tuned in properly.'

After the formalities the cruise passengers were directed to the motor launches waiting to take them to the air terminal, and an afternoon of sight-seeing in Venice before embarkation. As soon as they were settled, Molly produced a map.

'Look,' she said to Olivia, 'with any luck they'll take us through here and down the Grand Canal. My choice every time, whatever Charles says.'

'Otherwise we go round by the lagoon?'

'That's it. You've done your homework, I see.'

It was extremely pleasant to have arrived, and to sit relaxed in the sun with a holiday ahead. Olivia watched the launch filling up. The not-so-young predominated. An obviously academic couple were avoiding involvement. The man sat smoking a pipe, gazing straight ahead, while the woman immersed herself in a book with a Greek temple on the jacket. Two American couples, travelling together and hung around with photographic equipment, earnestly discussed their afternoon's programme.

'Soon as we've dahked, we head for Saint Mark's Square, then,' said one of the men, a serious type with rimless spectacles. 'That's sure OK by me.'

'I don't dispute for a moment that the Carpaccios in the Scuola di San Giorgio are his only cycle *in situ*,' a high cultured voice was saying, 'but should we cut out the Accademia altogether?'

'If we don't waste time hanging about here in the usual tiresome way, surely we can manage both. I suggest . . .'

Englishwomen Abroad, Olivia thought delightedly, observing sensible shoes, tweed suits and walking-sticks. I thought the type was extinct . . .

'. . . room for three people together here, surely?'

The speaker, an excitable well-dressed woman in late middle-age, was accompanied by a young couple, obviously embarrassed by the fuss she was making. Passengers already seated remained elaborately detached. Finally the two women found seats together, and the young man, addressed as Keith, came aft to a vacant seat near Olivia. To her relief he made no attempt to start a conversation. Although moderately long-haired he was at least clean in person, with a rather full heavy face. He looked intelligent, she thought.

7

The engine which had up to now been idling suddenly roared into life, and they were off at last.

'It *is* the Grand Canal,' Molly Moreton-Blake exclaimed triumphantly a few minutes later.

Olivia gazed enchanted at the panorama of sky and sea, and the scatter of small islands apparently floating on the water with campanili for masts. In spite of the bright sunshine the world was bathed in a softly muted light tinted with aquamarine and gold. Ahead the preposterous rickety skyline of the city added a final touch of fantasy.

'Murano,' Charles indicated with a wave, his thatch of white hair ruffled in the breeze as he resumed his seat after taking a photograph. 'Here and now I state categorically that I will not, repeat, not go over a glass factory when we're back here at the end of the cruise.'

'No one's asking you to, darling,' Molly replied soothingly.

'I'm allergic to factories,' Olivia assured him. 'I always dodge the WI visits to them at home.'

Charles Moreton-Blake saluted her with a characteristic lift of his hand. For twelve years after her husband's death, and for the purpose of giving her son David the best possible education, she had been the distinguished historian's secretary, a professional relationship which had developed into a lasting friendship with his wife and himself. He had fired her with some of his enthusiasms, and once David was launched she had retired to her cottage in the West Country, and become something of an authority on local history under his encouragement and guidance.

The volume of conversation in the launch was rising steadily. As they approached the white marble and cypress forest of the cemetery island of San Michelle one of the American party read aloud macabre details from a guide-book. His companions looked scandalized, and words such as 'prahblem' and 'cremation' floated aft. The Englishwomen Abroad exchanged pitying glances with raised eyebrows, and continued their discussion of Carpaccio's use of colour. The fussy woman had become tiresomely vivacious, and was making it clear to everyone within earshot that this was her third visit to Venice. As the launch nosed its way out into the Grand Canal she embarked on a running commentary.

'Why doesn't someone chuck her overboard?' Charles demanded as they passed under the Rialto Bridge. 'She'll be the cruise menace, buttonholing the unsuspecting to tell them her life history, and gatecrashing other people's conversations.'

Olivia glanced rather anxiously at the young man called Keith, but if he had overheard he gave no sign of it, sitting with his back half-turned and watching the palaces glide past. She noticed that the girl at the garrulous woman's side was looking at him with passionate intensity. She had long tawny hair, and the image of an uneasy lioness took shape in Olivia's mind. The babble all around rose to a crescendo as a fire-engine tore past, followed by an ambulance. Molly Moreton-Blake caught her eye and laughed.

'Bear up, my dear,' she exhorted her. 'They'll all vanish into thin air the moment we're on shore.'

Astonishingly the launch's voluble passengers did just this. On emerging from the boat station Olivia was swept by her friends up the narrow Calle Valaresso to get the incomparable view of St Mark's from the western end of the Piazza. She drew a deep breath, and from that moment neither saw nor thought of any of them for the rest of the afternoon.

Some two hours later the trio stood on the platform of the Clock Tower, weary but exhilarated, as the second bronze figure reverted to immobility with a jerk, and the resonant hum of the bell died away. In the great Piazza below holidaymakers circled and drifted, suggesting a crowd scene in a musical comedy. Shadows had begun to lengthen as the declining sun slanted shafts of gold from the north-west. A chilly little wind came creeping off the lagoon and up the Piazzetta. Molly knotted a scarf at her throat.

'Come on, let's go and have a ruinous hot cup of tea at Florian's,' she said. 'There are still some tables in the sun.'

They descended, and strolled across through the eddying crowd and the pools of pigeons. Sunny tables were in demand, but they managed to appropriate one as a couple got up and walked away. Olivia subsided thankfully on to a chair.

'What bliss,' she remarked, looking about her.

'Momento, signori.' A waiter dashed past bearing a laden tray on high.

Molly began to stack the used cups and plates.

'Anyone want to keep in touch?' she asked, holding up a *Daily Express* proclaiming industrial strife and decorated with pencilled sketches of passers-by and pigeons.

Her husband and Olivia declined vigorously as the waiter returned and swept everything from the table with expertise.

Across the Piazza the orchestra at Quadri's flung itself into a Strauss waltz. The crowds grew even more animated. A toddler, enchantingly dressed, staggered towards a posse of corn-gobbling pigeons with shouts of delight. The birds exploded into the air, circled smartly once and landed on the same spot to resume their eating. How can they cram in any more, Olivia wondered, looking at their bulging crops with some alarm.

The party lingered over tea, enjoying the ever-changing scene until it was time to make for the vaporetto which was to take them to the *Penelope*, berthed at San Basilio. A crowd was already waiting at the boat station. Olivia quickly spotted the Englishwomen Abroad leaning on their walking-sticks in a strategic position, and the four Americans looking somewhat exhausted. Before she could scan the assembly further a vaporetto was seen to be approaching, and there was general manoeuvring as a queue formed. Late arrivals on the scene like the Moreton-Blakes and herself had to wait for a second boat, and dusk was falling before they reached the white cliff-like side of the *Penelope*.

'What we want is a drink, if not two,' said Charles as they went wearily up the gangway. 'There's plenty of time. It's an informal buffet supper tonight, according to the book of words.'

Olivia was surprised and delighted by her cabin's comfort and seclusion. She felt that she would gladly forgo both drinks and buffet supper if only she could retire at once to the comfortable bed. It had been a wonderful but long day. However, a warning notice about boat drill put paid to any idea of the kind. Later, much restored by a brandy and tonic and some interesting food, she found herself sufficiently restored to enjoy a spell on deck, watching the lights of Venice slipping past and receding into the night.

Her bed was certainly very comfortable when she eventually reached it. She lay propped up against her pillows, book in hand and pervaded by a sense of well-being. Her thoughts touched happily on her son and daughter-in-law and small grandson whose London home she had left only that morning. Looking ahead, the prospect of a lazy day at sea on the morrow was attractive. Further ahead still was the excitement of seeing at last places which she had longed to visit: Athens, for instance, and Troy and Cnossos. All made possible by one of her modest holding of ten Premium Bonds incredibly winning a £500 prize.

The cabin was an outside one with a window on to the Promenade Deck. As she lay reading one or two people walked past, and she caught snatches of conversation, but soon the ship was quiet. She began to feel sleepy, switched off the bedside light and settled down for the night. The distant throb of the engines and the gentle roll of the *Penelope* was soporific, and she soon dozed off . . .

In her dream she could not see the man who was saying that it was so far, so good.

A woman's voice, half impatient, half mocking, was replying that he was an absolute clot: they'd barely taken off.

Bemused, Olivia struggled with the muddling idea that she was somehow back on the plane. Then she gave it up, and let sleep enfold her.

TWO

As the sun came up in a clear sky on the following morning the *Penelope* was progressing steadily down the Adriatic. Passengers with cabins on the port side tended to wake first as the bright light filtered in.

Drusilla Lang rubbed her eyes, stretched and lay thinking for a few moments in the lower berth of a double cabin on the Main Deck Aft. Then she got up quietly and tiptoed over to the porthole, shaking her tawny hair out of her eyes.

'I'm awake,' her husband Keith remarked from the upper berth. 'No, don't move—the combination of sun on your hair and that see-through thing you're wearing . . .'

He swung himself down, and took her in his arms.

'I do wish,' she said presently, as they stood gazing out of the porthole, 'that we were keeping closer to the Jugoslav coast. Everyone says how super it is, and we're too far out to see a thing.'

'As I've already said more than once,' he replied dryly, 'I expect damn all from this trip. In fact, I'm convinced it was a mistake to come.'

'It wasn't. We've had all this out before. You've been jolly ill,

11

you know. Pneumonia's no joke, even with antibiotics, and Dr Carmichael said you badly wanted sun and warmth. We ought to be able to count on that, anyway, and seeing all these places'll be good for your writing.'

Suddenly she burrowed her face into his neck.

'Oh, darling,' she said indistinctly, 'let's pretend for a minute that we're doing the trip on our own.'

In a single Boat Deck cabin with private shower, Mrs Audrey Vickers, Drusilla's aunt, was also indulging in imaginative thinking as she sipped the early morning tea brought by her steward. She lay back against the pillows, her restless dark eyes moving round the cabin. Without her make-up she looked every one of her fifty-five years.

She conjured up a scene ushered in by a light knock on the door.... In response to a gay summons to come in, Drusilla would appear on the threshold, bright-eyed and laughing, a metamorphosed Keith peeping over her shoulder in a charmingly deferential way, and asking if he might come too. Drusilla would stoop to kiss her affectionately, as they both enquired anxiously if she had slept well. Everything was absolutely super, they would assure her. As the blurbs said, the holiday of a lifetime ... Dear Aunt Audrey, how could they ever thank her enough for it all ...?

Uncannily, there actually were steps approaching, but they hurried past the cabin door and died away. Self-pity swept over Audrey Vickers, and gave way to hot indignation. After giving up her life to Drusilla, to be left for that lout Keith ...

She moistened her full, rather loose lips with the tip of her tongue, and her hand went out to a tin on the bedside table. She opened it and began to eat biscuits voraciously.

Dorothy Anstruther and Katherine Lingard, the English-women Abroad, were also enjoying early morning tea, although in more modest surroundings than those of Audrey Vickers. They could easily have afforded a more luxurious cabin, being spinsters of some substance, but their tradition and inclination was to plain living as well as high thinking. As they drank their tea they perused the programme for the day which had arrived with it.

'I shall go and hear this man Nalder on Greek Athletics,' Katherine Lingard announced. 'The sooner we find out if he's any use, the better. We don't want to waste time sitting out third-rate lectures.'

'I think I'll give him a trial too,' said her friend. 'Then, if only one can find a peaceful corner, I want to finish re-reading the Rieu Iliad. The other people don't look too bad on the whole. No beatniks or guitars, anyway.'

'I heard somebody say that tall man with untidy white hair and two women in tow is C. Moreton-Blake, the historian.'

'If he is, I was at Newnham with his sister. They might be worth cultivating.'

Olivia Strode, not an early tea addict, slept on in her starboard cabin until comings and goings outside woke her just before eight o'clock. She spent a few minutes enjoying the prospect of a day without commitments and responsibilities. A fine day, too. Quivers of sunlight reflected from the water danced on the wall. Presently she got up, dressed in a leisurely way, and went in search of the dining-saloon. The Moreton-Blakes, already breakfasting, waved from a far corner.

'You sit anywhere you like for breakfast,' Molly told her as she joined them. 'We shan't know the worst about our permanent table companions until lunch. Did you sleep all right?'

'Like a log,' Olivia replied. 'All the same, I'm looking forward to lazing on deck most of the day. I think I'll go to the lecture this morning, though.'

'I've reconnoitred,' Charles reported, 'and there's plenty of deck space and chairs to suit all types of anatomy. Altogether we seem to be pretty well found.'

'You can risk coffee if you want to,' his wife added as the steward came up. 'It's surprisingly good.'

The morning slipped away pleasantly, with a useful and entertaining lecture sandwiched between two spells of idling in the sun. Arriving for lunch a few minutes ahead of the Moreton-Blakes, Olivia found two strangers converging on the table to which her party had been assigned, an English couple whom she placed in the mid-thirties. Quite handsome and decidedly with-it, she thought, glancing at the tall blonde woman's smart cruise-wear and skilfully applied make-up. The man, also tall and blond sported a royal blue towelling shirt and a pair of light trousers, and her immediate reaction was that she liked him the better of the two. He had a more relaxed and rather humorous face. They both greeted her in a friendly way, introducing

13

themselves as Lorna and John Bayley. As small talk got going some teasing recollection stirred at the back of her mind, but the arrival of the Moreton-Blakes and another couple distracted her. But when everyone was settled she remembered.

'Do you know, I think we almost met in the Piazza yesterday afternoon,' she said to the Bayleys. 'About half-past four, at Florian's. We came along hoping for a table in the sun, and two people got up and left just at the right moment. We were so grateful: our legs were giving way under us.'

'My God, don't I know that feeling!' Lorna Bayley exclaimed. 'This compulsive sightseeing nearly kills you, and yet you daren't stop in case you never get to the place again. I gave out for the moment after St Mark's, though, and insisted on a tea-break, so it probably was us.'

'Since nobody else is saying what an extraordinary coincidence, I'll say it myself.' John Bayley grinned at Olivia. 'A good spot, the Piazza, isn't it? I could sit there all day watching the crowds, and absorbing that incredible façade of the Basilica.'

'Florian's knows how to cash in on the free spectacle,' remarked Lorna. 'Everyone says the coffee's just as good and half the price just round the corner.'

'Overheads,' said Charles-Moreton Blake. 'Their rates must be colossal.'

Lunch was a success. The food and service were voted good, and the noise-level in the dining-saloon tolerable. Olivia reflected that they had been lucky in their table-mates. John Bayley in particular was agreeable and amusing, and the older couple, a Mr and Mrs Mayling, innocuous if dull.

After coffee in one of the lounges the Moreton-Blakes announced that they were going off to their cabin for a siesta. Rather glad of the chance of some time on her own, Olivia prospected carefully and finally settled herself in a secluded spot on the Boat Deck with a copy of *Emma*. For a time she gazed contentedly out to sea, and then began to read and became absorbed, only subconsciously aware of other arrivals in the area round her.

Suddenly the noisy dragging of a chair across the deck to within a few feet of her own roused her. Glancing up irritably, to her dismay she recognized the garrulous woman of the launch, and hastily immersed herself in her book again. But she found it impossible to concentrate. There were sounds of annoyance: mutterings, thumpings of cushions and sighs clearly

14

intended to attract attention. Finally a spectacle case clattered to the ground, shot under her own chair, and emerged on the other side. Picking it up and returning it to its owner could not possibly be avoided. As she feared, this courtesy at once sparked off a torrent of speech.

'How *very* kind—thank you a thousand times. *So* clumsy of me! I know how annoying it is to be disturbed when one is reading. I'm a great reader myself—I'm so much alone, you know, and it helps to pass the time, doesn't it? That and TV. What *should* we do without TV? I really had to move over to this side, out of the sun. So thoughtless of my young people to put me in such an unsuitable place, and then disappear before I had time to try it out. I had to get all my bits and pieces over here by myself. They really might have waited to see if I was all right before they went off. I'm standing them the entire cost of this holiday, and as you know, these good cruises are not exactly cheap ... Do let me make amends for disturbing you by offering you one of these.'

Olivia politely declined the proffered box of chocolates, made a casual remark about the weather and resumed her reading. Of course she would have to move to somewhere else. It was absolutely impossible to relax knowing that this infuriating woman would burst out into conversation at any moment. How soon could she decently get up and go?

Her hesitation was fatal.

'You're Mrs Strode, aren't you?' demanded her neighbour.

Really, this was the end. Slightly turning her head, Olivia admitted that she was.

'May I introduce myself? I'm Audrey Vickers—Mrs Vickers. I noticed you on the launch, and again at lunch today, with that distinguished-looking elderly man and his pretty wife. He's Professor Moreton-Blake, isn't he? I looked you all up on the table list outside the dining-saloon ... I'm sure you must be thinking that I'm very curious. I'm not, you know. Not in any horrid sense, that is. It's just that I'm so interested in people. I expect it's because I'm so lonely since my niece's marriage. She married so dreadfully young. It's left the most terrible blank in my life. I brought her up, you see. She was tragically left an orphan at four. I had recently lost my husband, and I took in the poor little mite and positively gave up my life to her. We were such companions ...'

Mrs Vickers' voice mercifully trailed off.

Olivia, exasperated with herself for not having made a speedier getaway, observed non-committally that people were marrying younger these days.

'In some ways I think it's a very good thing,' she added.

'Ah!'

Although somewhat muffled by a second chocolate, the exclamation rang with self-vindicating triumph. The next moment Audrey Vickers was in full cry, gripping the arms of her deck chair as she leant towards Olivia.

'As you say, Mrs Strode, a good thing *in some ways*. And in *some cases*, no doubt. But certainly not in Drusilla's. Her unfortunate marriage is a tragedy. A sheer undiluted tragedy.'

Hardly pausing to take breath she poured out an impassioned narrative shot through and through with self-pity. Drusilla, left a virtually penniless orphan, had been educated at a leading girls' public school at her aunt's expense. There she had done brilliantly, yes, brilliantly, winning a scholarship to Oxford. The additional cost of a university education had not been grudged for a moment. More academic triumphs had followed. Drusilla had taken a First in science, and been offered a postgraduate research year.

'Imagine my feelings, Mrs Strode, when I suddenly got a letter to say that she had declined this splendid offer, married this creature Keith Lang in a registry office and taken a post to teach chemistry in a technical college – some sort of trade school, as far as I can make out – so that he could concentrate on his writing. Writing!' Mrs Vickers infused a world of scorn into the word. 'Simply an excuse to avoid doing a proper job. He's bone idle. Of course he saw the chance of getting a silly infatuated girl to keep him, and leapt at it. But it was Drusilla's deceit that wounded me so cruelly. Hiding it all from me after I'd given up my life to her, and simply presenting me with a fait accompli. It's beyond all belief!'

On the contrary, it's entirely understandable in the light of your frenzied possessiveness, Olivia thought. Before she could speak, however, Mrs Vickers hurried on again. In spite of the shameful way in which Drusilla had treated her, she had done everything possible to help the young couple. She had even offered to make Drusilla an allowance, which had quite incredibly been declined. However the pair had deigned to accept this expensive holiday, on the grounds that Keith needed a period of convalescence after what was said to be pneumonia. Such nonsense: everyone had had flu last winter, and taken no notice of it. It was Drusilla who needed a rest and change. She had been worn out doing an exhausting teaching job, and looking after a husband who simply traded on her ridiculous infatuation for him.

Watching the convulsive movement of Mrs Vickers' throat as she talked, and the restless twisting and untwisting of her hands, Olivia felt disquieted. The woman would be under treatment in a mental hospital soon if she didn't take herself in hand. While realizing that it was almost certainly wasted effort, she broke in on a further tirade.

'You know, Mrs Vickers,' she said, 'a lot of rubbish is talked about the generation gap, but it does exist and one's got to accept it. Young people these days have different values. Drusilla is obviously very intelligent, and she's thought things out, and come to the conclusion that she'll find sharing Keith's life and work more satisfying than going all out for an academic career of her own. After all, it's her happiness you want, isn't it?'

Mrs Vickers stared at her in outraged incomprehension.

'You can't possibly have brought up a child yourself to talk like this. You simply don't understand what it means to part with one.'

'On the contrary, I understand very well indeed. I was left a widow with a son of ten, and worked to educate him and get him a good start in life. We were companions just as you say you and Drusilla were. But above everything I hoped he'd marry a girl he loved, and make his own life, although this would obviously mean the end of ours together. And I was immensely thankful when it happened. I do hope that you will come to feel the same about your niece,' Olivia added, feeling entirely unconvinced. 'And now I really must go and find my friends. They'll be wondering where I have got to.'

There was no reply. She gathered up her belongings in a stony silence, and departed, intending to take refuge in her cabin. On the way down she was unexpectedly hailed by the Englishwomen Abroad, who were reclining in deckchairs with books.

'In need of care and protection?' enquired Dorothy Anstruther. 'Join us if you care to. We came up to the Boat Deck and saw the Vickers menace holding forth to you.'

'She sits at our table with those two unfortunate young

17

things, God help them and us,' said Katherine Lingard, looking up from the Iliad. 'So far we've managed to choke her off, though. Here's a chair. No need to talk,' she added pointedly.

Amused, Olivia thanked them, and sat down. It was certainly much nicer to stay on deck. For a time she thought about the Vickers–Lang situation with mingled indignation and compassion. Then she shook herself mentally, and picked up her own book. There was nothing she could do to help, and it was futile to let other people's problems spoil her holiday to no purpose.

The random selection of humanity which had embarked on the *Penelope* soon developed a corporate identity with a life rhythm. The latter was punctuated by such communal activities as meals, lectures about places to be visited and the shore excursions to these. Within the group as a whole, however, numerous smaller units emerged. Some of these were based on shared interests. The spring flowers of Greece were at the height of their glory, and dedicated botanists conferred enthusiastically, and sought each other out in the evenings for prolonged inquests on the day's bag of specimens. To the ornithologists the classical sites visited were primarily the habitats of exciting and unfamiliar birds, whose identities were the subject of endless serious discussion. Social sub-groups were also swift to emerge. A few owners of titles and members of the higher ranks of the services hastily coalesced into a self-constituted élite, and derived immense satisfaction from their membership, confining their intercourse with outsiders to gracious politeness. A minor playwright attracted a coterie bent on using his Christian name as loudly and frequently as possible. The academics accorded each other due recognition, and conversed together in the manner of fellow countrymen on alien territory. A handful of people who had joined the cruise under a misapprehension as to its character went about looking disgruntled, and complaining about the lack of entertainment on board. The great majority of the passengers, however, were genuinely interested in some aspect of the classical world, and enjoyed themselves thoroughly, finding plenty of common ground for making pleasant acquaintances.

No one had a more agreeable time than Olivia Strode. She revelled in the complete freedom from her usual chores, in the perfect weather, and in the interest and beauty of places which she had always wanted to visit. Her only regret was that the days passed so swiftly, and on the morning of the *Penelope*'s arrival off Delos she realized sadly that two-thirds of the holiday was already over.

As the small landing-craft approached the jetty she forgot to repine: the island cast its spell over her. The sapphire of sea and sky framed the dazzling white marble ruins and the enchanting little peak of Mount Cynthus, and the landscape seemed bathed in light and peace. Olivia was glad that she had come on ahead of her friends: she would have a little time alone in this heavenly place. She made her way slowly towards the assembly point in the old Slave Market, and sat down on a low wall, blissfully happy.

After a time, however, the steady stream of later arrivals became a distraction. There was talking and laughter all around her, and cameras clicked endlessly. She watched the Maylings conscientiously referring to their guide-book. Not far away Lorna Bayley in emerald green slacks and a bikini-type top was sitting perched on a mound, against which John was leaning as he lit a cigarette. Olivia watched Audrey Vickers suddenly bear down on them, with a reluctant Drusilla and Keith Lang in the rear. Her habit of thrusting her company on people was by now recognized as a cruise hazard, and this time she had got the Bayleys trapped. She addressed herself to John, talking excitedly with a wealth of gesture. He was shaking his head, and appeared to be making a series of vigorous denials. Finally Lorna descended from her perch, and he contrived to disengage himself, raising his eyes to heaven as they walked past Olivia. She reciprocated, and then seeing the Moreton-Blakes coming along the path from the jetty, got up and went to meet them.

In retrospect she came to look back on the morning at Delos as both the highlight and the turning point of her cruise. It had a dreamlike beauty, yet left impressions sharply etched in her memory. The Avenue of Lions, for instance, and the Palm of Leda, the solitary beach beyond ablaze with flowers to the water's edge, the grim Herm, and the superb cat rampant in the mosaic floor of a house in the Graeco-Roman quarter. All these and other things remained with her, crowned by the incomparable view of the Cyclades from the summit of Mount Cynthus.

During lunch the *Penelope* made the short crossing from Delos to Mykonos. The first intimation that the morning had been a turning point came when passengers emerged from the dining-saloon. The brightness of the day was already partly eclipsed by a fine web of high cloud advancing over the sky from the south-east. Olivia exclaimed in dismay.

'The weather can't be going to break!'

'Can't it?' said Charles Moreton-Blake. 'You don't realize how lucky we've been up to now, my dear. I talked to a chap yesterday who'd done the trip a couple of years ago, and they only had four decent days in a fortnight.'

That afternoon Olivia found an expedition disappointing for the first time. Colour had drained out of the world leaving a sense of drabness. But under any circumstances, she thought, Mykonos would have seemed an anticlimax after Delos. She was not attracted by its picturesqueness, which struck her as cultivated and unconvincing, and the Moreton-Blakes agreed with her. They strolled along the crowded waterfront with its cafés and tourist shops, and came on the Englishwomen Abroad, leaning on their walking-sticks and looking around critically.

'Tarted up,' summarized Katherine Lingard. 'Try the churches. There are one or two quite good icons.'

'Anything but those damned windmills up there,' said Charles.

After a brief tour of the little town they made for a café, and were hailed by the Bayleys.

'Join us,' invited John. 'The tea's lousy, but at least it's hot and wet.'

It was not a particularly cheerful little party. Lorna Bayley seemed out of sorts, and conversation soon flagged.

'I can't think why the hell they brought us in here,' John remarked. 'The place is positively twee.'

'Some people are managing to enjoy it. anyway,' Lorna retorted. 'For goodness sake stop grousing. Come and buy me a non-souvenir at one of the shops instead.'

Still grumbling he was led off. By common consent the Moreton-Blakes and Olivia queued for the first boat back to the *Penelope*, which was to sail for Athens that same evening.

For many of the passengers the day in Athens was the chief attraction of the cruise, and there was general disappointment that it dawned overcast and sultry. Contemplating a depressing view of Piraeus from her cabin, Olivia Strode realized that she had a headache, an unusual occurence in her robustly healthy life. She remembered that her daughter-in-law had pressed a box containing a few simple medicaments on her, and unearthed and took two aspirin before facing breakfast in the dining-saloon.

The change in the weather seemed to have put a damper on people's spirits. A report went round that *Penelope* was berthed close to a large American cruise ship, and there were groans from experienced travellers.

'We shan't be able to hear ourselves think on the Acropolis with every guide in the place bellowing his head off,' John Bayley remarked gloomily.

Molly Moreton-Blake suggested hopefully that the Americans might have 'done' Athens the day before, and be going out of the city on excursions, but this optimism met with little response. Later, the dreary drive from Piraeus still further lowered the temperature. It was not until she was walking up the steep Processional Way that Olivia's imagination was suddenly fired by the scale and splendour of the Propylaea. A few moments later the exquisite little Temple of the Wingless Victory moved her so deeply that she lingered to gaze, letting the Moreton-Blakes go on ahead.

If only there wasn't such a crowd, she thought, almost jostled off her feet by an avalanche of Greek students preceded by a bearded professor. The next moment she realized to her dismay that Audrey Vickers and the Langs were on her heels, and hurried on up the slope pointedly unaware of them. At the top she found her way blocked by an excited huddle of Americans. Three smart women, apparently long-separated college contemporaries, were talking at once, introducing the husbands acquired since campus days.

'If this isn't a real thrill, girls...'

'I'll have you all meet John B. Harrigan...'

'You don't say! The war sure got the boys moving around...'

'Why, honey, I said, the future's right here, over this side. Take it from me, Amurrican citizenship...'

'Excuse me,' Olivia pushed her way past the group with uncharacteristic vigour, to achieve her first sight of the Parthenon amid inappropriate feelings of irritation. She moved over to her right to put a safe distance between herself and the Vickers party.

As she stood and looked her annoyance suddenly died, and she became quite oblivious of both crowds and noise. After a timeless interval her eyes moved to the Erectheum, and the matchless beauty of the caryatids drew her towards it. But she

21

had taken only a few steps when an agitated and angry voice broke in on her thoughts. Glancing round involuntarily she saw Audrey Vickers, seated on a fallen column with her left hand clutching the region of her heart. She was flushed, and indignantly addressing the Langs who stood in front of her with an air of helplessness.

'I tell you that I must go straight back to the ship—at once, and you must take me. I can't possibly manage by myself. How can you even suggest it, Drusilla? I feel most unwell. The dreadful struggle up here was far too much for my heart. We should have been warned how taxing it was. Most remiss—I shall certainly complain.'

One look at the young Lang's agonized faces precipitated Olivia into action.

'Can't I help?' she asked, joining the group. 'I'll gladly see you back to the ship in a taxi, Mrs Vickers, and then Mr and Mrs Lang needn't miss time up here.'

She registered glances of hopeless gratitude from Drusilla and Keith, and of positive venom from Mrs Vickers.

'Thank you,' the latter snapped, 'But I prefer the help of my relatives. Come along.' She stood up, pointedly turning her back on Olivia.

Of all the unmitigated bitches, the latter thought, walking away and biting her lip in indignation. Catching sight of the Moreton-Blakes, she returned their wave and went towards them.

'Heart my foot!' Charles commented on hearing her story. 'Indigestion, if I know anything. The woman eats like a horse, and is always stuffing herself with chocolates between meals into the bargain. I hope those unfortunate youngsters get back here.'

At the end of the morning the cruise passengers were taken back to the *Penelope* for lunch, at which Mrs Vickers did not appear. The Langs seemed to be under a concerted attack from their table companions. Afterwards it became known that their aunt had cancelled the bookings for the afternoon visit to the National Museum, and the drive to Sunion afterwards, saying that she felt far too unwell to be left alone. Dorothy Anstruther and Katherine Lingard in particular had protested that there was not the slightest need for Drusilla and Keith to remain on board. There was a telephone in the cabin, a ship's doctor and a nurse. The doctor had been completely reassuring, and merely advised Mrs Vickers to spend the afternoon quietly.

'It was no go,' Katherine Lingard said. 'They just wouldn't play. All I can say is that if they're after her money in the long term, it's dear at the price, however much she's got.'

Olivia's headache was still grumbling away in the background, and she found the crowds and reverberating noise in the National Museum exhausting. When, at the end of the visit, the Moreton-Blakes suggested cutting out the Sunion expedition, she agreed with relief, and after returning to the ship and enjoying a peaceful cup of tea, she retired to her cabin for a rest.

Most of the passengers were ashore, and it was blessedly quiet. Lying on her bed she was surprised to find that the prospect of the end of the cruise had become attractive. Was it the sudden lack of sunshine, or the fact that Mykonos had been a flop, and Athens, taken as a whole, a bit disappointing? Or was it that she felt both mentally and physically rather tired? A bit of all three, probably, she decided. And people being on top of one on board ship, nice though most of them were.

Dinner re-echoed with the laments of those who had been on the Sunion excursion. It appeared that the coast was being ruined by building, and the sunset had been invisible behind thick cloud. To crown everything it had been dark for most of the way back. Even the normally cheerful John Bayley seemed still afflicted by his gloom of the previous afternoon.

'The whole thing was a washout,' Lorna agreed. 'I wish to goodness we'd stayed in Athens and had a look at the shops. What on earth's this?'

At her abrupt change of tone everyone looked up to see a steward handing her an envelope on a salver.

'A radiogram for you, madam,' he told her.

Looking startled, she ripped it open and read it.

'My God,' she exclaimed. 'It only wanted something like this to round off the day!'

She pushed the paper across to John, who raised his eyebrows and whistled.

'Just to say that a house Lorna's had left her's been burnt down,' he informed the company, who were trying to look politely unconcerned.

There was a chorus of commiseration.

'Does it mean that you'll have to go straight back instead of having your week in Venice?' Molly Moreton-Blake asked sympathetically.

The Bayleys looked at each other.

'I don't really see why, do you?' said Lorna. 'After all, it's a solicitor's job to cope with this sort of thing. He knows about it—he sent the radiogram. Surely he'll have the sense to get on to the insurance people?'

'We could ring him when we get in to Venice, I suppose.'

'Anyone living in the place?' asked Charles Moreton-Blake.

'No, thank goodness,' Lorna told him. 'We were trying to sell it. It was furnished after a fashion, but we'd removed anything of value. It belonged to my godmother, who died recently at the age of ninety-seven, so you can just imagine what the clearing-up was like. She'd lived there most of her life.'

The conversation turned to possible causes of fire in unoccupied houses. Olivia thought of Poldens, her much-loved cottage in the West Country, and felt a chill. It was thatched . . .

'Do you realize that the young Langs aren't in to dinner?' Charles said later. 'Somebody was saying in the bar that they sent in a note to the Vickers after lunch, saying they'd be out for the rest of the day, and that she went up in hysterics. Glad they had the sense and the guts.'

This news was acclaimed by the whole table, and opinions of Mrs Vickers were freely expressed.

'I should think everyone on board knows by now that she's paying for the Langs,' John Bayley remarked. 'Stuck 'em down about the cheapest cabin there is, too.'

Remembering the morning's incident on the Acropolis, Olivia felt a passing uneasiness. Had it been a case of the last straw? She detested rows. But anyway, it really wasn't her business. On a sudden impulse she invited everybody to an after-dinner drink.

This turned out to be a good idea, and a morale-raiser at the end of a not particularly successful day. The Bayleys seemed philosophical over the fire, and a much more cheerful atmosphere developed. Presently someone reported that the weather was looking up, and before turning in the party went out on deck to look at the harbour lights and get a breath of fresh air. A pleasant cool breeze was clearing the sky, and Olivia stayed for a few final turns round the Promenade Deck on her own. The ship was due to sail at midnight, and the ordered bustle of departure had begun. People who had dined in Athens were returning in taxis and coming up the gangway, and a tug was already in the offing. She strolled about in a leisurely way, pausing from time to time to lean on the rail and watch the various activities in progress. It was during one of these pauses in the after part of the ship that she realized that a conversation was going on just out of sight. The next moment she recognized Drusilla Lang's voice, speaking with passionate intensity.

'I'll never forgive her for what she said to you Keith—never! This time it really is the end. She can leave her bloody money to a cats' home if she likes. From the moment we get back, I'm through. I'll never see her, or write or speak to her again. If she rings, I'll just leave the receiver off.'

'It doesn't bother me in the slightest, as I've often said before. In fact, it's interesting from the psychological angle.'

'There's a limit, and we've got to it. I hate her! If only she really had a weak heart instead of pretending, and using it to blackmail people who are fools enough to be taken in. Anyway, she can't stop me getting the money my grandfather left when she does die, and the sooner she does, the better.'

Olivia moved quietly away, feeling depressed. There must have been an appalling row. Probably Drusilla was right, and a complete break was the only possible solution, but how impossible human beings were. So absolutely blind about themselves. And there was something so sterile about hatred.

The last days of the cruise melted away, bringing a feeling that a way of life was running down. The *Penelope* called at Pylos, and there was a visit to the site of Eglianos. Thereafter the ship ploughed steadily northwards towards Venice, and although the sun was shining again a cooler element had crept into the weather. It was observed that a definite break had taken place between Mrs Vickers and the Langs. The former kept a good deal to her cabin, and unavoidable encounters at meals were conducted with stiff politeness.

'There's a nasty look in the Vickers woman's eye,' Dorothy Anstruther remarked. 'I forecast a visit to her solicitor to make a new will as soon as she gets home.'

The ship's arrival at Venice was timed to allow a full day's sightseeing and a final night on board before the return flight to London. Various excursions had been organized, but the Moreton-Blakes bore Olivia off for a programme of their own choosing. The morning went in a fascinating stroll across the city, taking in lively fish and flower markets, the great church of San Zanipolo with its absorbing monuments, and the Colleoni

25

statue which seemed to challenge the world from the quiet little piazza outside. From the Fondamenta Nuove they took the vaporetto to Torcello, ate delectably and expensively at Cipriani's as a final fling and wandered in the timelessness of the island and its emotive cathedral all through the warm spring afternoon. Later, by changing boats at the Fondamenta, they returned to the *Penelope* by water in the magic of the evening light.

Arriving rather late for dinner they found a depleted table.

'The poor Bayleys have had to go straight back to London after all,' Mrs Mayling told them. 'Isn't it unfortunate for them? They thought they had better ring their solicitor when we got in this morning, and he seems to have felt quite strongly that they should go.'

'I suppose they'll be let in for a lot of bother over the insurance, and what-have-you,' said Molly Moreton-Blake.

'They were lucky to get seats on a plane at such short notice,' remarked her husband.

THREE

As soon as the *Penelope* docked at Venice early on Monday, 30 April, her passengers' corporate identity had begun to disintegrate. A few of them, like the Bayleys, left the ship that morning, forgoing their last night on board. Others trickled away after breakfast on Tuesday to make their own way to various destinations. The organized exodus to the airport soon followed, where two chartered VC10s were waiting to convey the party back to London. The final dispersal took place from Heathrow in the early afternoon amid preoccupied farewells and hurried waves.

Olivia Strode was soon heading for Wimbledon, driven by her daughter-in-law Julian. She turned to eye her critically.

'You look the absolute picture of health, in spite of all this dashing about with the baby due in a matter of weeks.'

Julian laughed.

'I feel fine, just as I did with Rupert. You'll find him in top form, but it's time he had a brother or sister, you know. He's beginning to throw his weight about.'

Mrs Vickers and the langs had been obliged to fly back to

London in the same aircraft because of the pre-allocation of seats, an uncomfortable journey ending in a stiff parting on landing, and sedulous avoidance of each other in the arrival lounge and at the customs. Eventually Mrs Vickers drove off in a taxi to catch a mid-afternoon train for Highcastle at Waterloo. She did not offer the young people a lift, although Waterloo was also the station for Fulminster where they lived. They had already decided on a later train, and boarded an airport bus with their luggage.

Audrey Vickers lived at Redbay, a small coastal resort fifteen miles from Highcastle. Her house, Lauriston, was a pleasant one of pre-war vintage near the sea front. She had little eye for its amenities on her return, however, being in a tense state of anger and vindictiveness. As Dorothy Anstruther had correctly foreseen, she lost no time in contacting her solicitors, Messrs Partridge, Webster and Partridge of Highcastle. Greatly to her annoyance she learnt that the senior partner who handled her affairs was away on the firm's business, and would not be available until Friday morning. She felt it a further outrage that the action she had in mind should be held up in this way, and any acquaintance she chanced to meet was pinned down and forced to listen to the saga of her grievances. Her daily woman, a Mrs Young, was subjected to lengthy tirades on the ingratitude of Drusilla and Keith, but being phlegmatic by temperament and well accustomed to them, she merely let it all wash over her as she went about her work. At home she remarked to her husband that the holiday looked like having made things worse instead of better between Mrs V and the young 'uns.

Anger, self-pity and frustration are all exhausting and deterrents to sleep. On Thursday night Audrey Vickers tossed and turned into the small hours, and then unadvisedly took a second sleeping-pill. As a result she did not hear her alarm clock go off at seven-thirty, and woke just before nine to find that she had barely time to dress and snatch a cup of coffee before starting for her appointment in Highcastle. Having scrawled a hasty note to Mrs Young, she left the house ten minutes behind schedule, and was delayed further by unusually heavy traffic on the road. On arrival in the city she failed to notice a 'No Entry' sign which had gone up a few days previously, and was instantly swooped on by a police officer. He was unmoved by her indignant protest that she had only just returned from abroad.

'Forgotten how to read while you've been on holiday, madam?' he enquired sarcastically. 'Let me take a look at your licence, please.'

She sat fuming as he inspected it in a leisurely manner.

'My driving licence is perfectly in order. I've got a most urgent appointment, and I'm late already.'

'You're lucky not to have an appointment at the Casualty Department at the hospital, madam. Reverse now, and I'll see you out of here. And please drive with proper care and attention in future. I shall have to report this incident, of course.'

Eventually she reached her destination, breathless, taut and nearly a quarter of an hour late.

Mr Richard Partridge, a heavy-faced man with small sagacious eyes and grey hair receding from his temples, rose to greet her and extended a welcoming hand. Mrs Vickers was in the difficult client category, and observing storm signals, he made polite enquiries about her recent holiday.

Audrey Vickers cut into these with scant courtesy, hardly waiting to sit down before embarking on a recital of her grievances.

'Thanks to Drusilla's abominable treatment of me—and her dreadful husband's too, of course—that goes without saying— the cruise has been an absolute misery, Mr Partridge. I paid every penny for both of them out of my own pocket—every penny, let me tell you, and what did I get in return? I got continual disagreeableness and no sign of appreciation for all that I was doing for them, the most outrageous neglect when I collapsed from doing too much solely for their sakes, and when I ventured to protest from my bed of sickness, Drusilla was grossly abusive. Well, this time they're going to find that they've gone too far. The worm will turn, as the saying goes, and I've come to my turning point at last. I want you to draw up a fresh will for me. Those two needn't think they're going to enjoy my money when I'm gone.'

As Audrey Vickers paused for breath Mr Partridge, adept at playing for time, took off his spectacles and swung them gently to and fro, while resting his right elbow on his desk.

'I think we had better have a look at your present will,' he said, flicking a switch and speaking to his secretary.

'My new one is to be entirely different. I've devoted a great deal of thought to it, and I'm perfectly clear——'

'Quite,' interposed Mr Partridge, who had been suddenly

visited by a bizarre idea. 'By the way, when you took over Drusilla as a child, you didn't legally adopt her, did you?'

Audrey Vickers stared at him.

'Adopt her? No. I was her legal guardian under her mother's will, and as such I consider it was outrageous that the County Council insisted on sending people to see if she was being cared for properly. That sort of thing was intended for quite a different class—it was insulting. As you know, I accepted the commitments, gave up my whole life——'

'Mrs Vickers' will, Mr Partridge.' A brisk man materialized, placed a document in front of his employer and vanished again

'As I was saying, I gave up my whole life to Drusilla. I can't see what difference it makes whether I adopted her or not,' Audrey Vickers concluded fretfully.

'Had you done so,' replied Mr Partridge, watching her narrowly, 'or had she been your own child, she might conceivably have had ground for contesting a will of yours which made no provision for her.'

He decided that her reaction was merely one of impatience, and dismissed his bizarre idea.

'There's no point in discussing it, surely? How soon can you have my new will ready for me to sign?'

'That rather depends on its provisions,' Mr Partridge said, running his eyes down the sheets of typescript in front of him. 'Do I understand that you do not intend Drusilla to benefit at all?'

'I'm not leaving her one farthing,' Audrey Vickers replied, disregarding the disappearance of this coin from the currency of the realm. 'All my life I've been imposed on and exploited... I've decided to leave what there is when I go—and I'm not going to scrimp and save, I can tell you—to charities to help elderly people. I expect there are hundreds who've been made use of, and then been thrown on the rubbish heap as I have. People who are getting on ought to be protected from this idle, heartless modern generation. You can find some suitable charities for me, I suppose?'

'We can.' Mr Partridge made some notes on a pad. 'I had better get some detailed information about half a dozen or so, and you can look through it and make a choice.'

'I don't want a lot of delay. The sooner all this is settled, the better. The worry and upset of it all is making me quite ill.'

Still writing, Mr Partridge observed his client's restless

changes of posture, and the nervous movements of her hands. He had known Drusilla from a child, and her marriage and the manner of it had not surprised him at all. He decided to take a calculated risk.

'The step you are proposing to take is a very radical one, Mrs Vickers,' he observed carefully laying down his pen.

'Are you suggesting that I don't know my own mind, or that I'm not in a fit state mentally to make a will?' she blazed at him. 'If you don't want to deal with my affairs, Mr Partridge, I can easily go elsewhere. There are plenty of other solicitors in High-castle who would be ready to take them over, and even to give me a little sympathy. All through this dreadful business of Drusilla's marriage you've always been on her side and against me— I'm well aware of that.'

Mr Partridge had no intention of allowing any development of this kind. Quite apart from the loss of a client, it would not be in Drusilla Lang's interests. In Mrs Vickers' present over-wrought state it was reasonable to feel that she might change her mind once again about the disposition of her state.

'I can assure you,' he replied, 'that from the time when you first placed your affairs in my hands, I have consistently tried to further your interests. If you wish me to draw up a will for you on the lines you've indicated, I'm ready to do so.'

'Very well,' she snapped, sounding little mollified. 'I don't want any more changes in my unhappy life. Only do get it done as soon as possible. Choose any charities you like of the kind I've described: I don't care which. I've far too much on my mind to bother about details like that. Now, the other thing I want you to do for me is to find out the name of a really good and reliable enquiry agent.'

Long years of professional discipline enabled Mr Partridge to conceal any sign of surprise. That chap Lang, he thought quickly . . . She must think she can get hold of something which might bust up the marriage . . . Drugs?

'A local man?' he enquired.

'Oh no, certainly not anyone local. You know how things leak out. Someone in London, preferably. I can run up quite easily to discuss my business.'

She spoke with a finality which made it clear that she had no intention of revealing the nature of her business. Mr Partridge made another note, and looked up to see her gathering her gloves and handbag together.

'Be sure to telephone me at once when you have found me someone, and when my will is ready for signature,' she adjured him as they both got up.

Returning to his room after seeing Audrey Vickers off, Mr Partridge sat for a moment staring at his notes. If she were really hoping to wreck Drusilla's marriage as well as cutting her out of the will, it really was a bit thick, he thought. Just how bloody-minded can you get?

Meanwhile, on stepping out of Partridge, Webster and Partridge's Office, Audrey Vickers realized that she was feeling faint and slightly giddy. She panicked in a swirl of self-pity, visualizing a collapse from heart failure in a public street, an ambulance called by a passer-by and a hospital bed with no next-of-kin to call upon. Then the more prosaic thought that she had been obliged to miss her normal cooked breakfast reassured her, and she set off in quest of elevenses. A pot of coffee, a plate of toothsome cakes and a friendly greeting from a well-known waitress soon restored her. As she ate and drank with enjoyment even her indignation with Mr Partridge began to subside. All men were the same, she told herself. Changing her solicitor wouldn't make any difference. Drusilla was young and personable, and there it was.

She debated staying in Highcastle for a look round the shops, and having lunch there, but finally decided to return home when she had bought one or two things from a delicatessen to supplement the cold chicken in the refrigerator. After lunch she would have a good rest on her bed. She needed one after such a shocking night.

The drive back to Redbay was accomplished without mishap. After garaging the car, Audrey Vickers let herself into Lauriston. Mrs Young had come and gone, leaving a silent tidy house, and the midday post on the chest in the hall, two receipts, a circular and a smallish flat parcel neatly done up with Sellotape. It had a London postmark and was correctly addressed in block capitals. Unable to place it, Audrey Vickers tugged at the Sellotape. As she at last managed to pull off the outer wrapping a printed slip fell to the ground. She picked it up and recognized the familiar motif of a Greek long ship of the Homeric Age riding the waves. Under it was the legend 'With the compliments of Odyssey Tours Ltd'. The box, she was delighted to find, contained chocolates by Honeydew, a small firm well known for its luxury class confectionery. It slid open in the manner of a matchbox. Only a half-pound box, she thought. Really, considering what we paid ... still, it's a nice idea, even if it's only an advertisement. Marchpane Magic, too ... I've had them before. Better not spoil my lunch, perhaps. They'll be lovely when I go up to rest and have a look at the paper. Reluctantly she put the chocolates down and set about getting herself a meal.

In spite of her elevenses Audrey Vickers made a good lunch. She was feeling more cheerful than at any time since her return from the cruise now that she had given Mr Partridge his instructions. The phrase pleaded her, and she repeated it to herself several times as she stacked crockery and cutlery in the dishwasher, and also rehearsed her opening conversation with the enquiry agent whom Mr Partridge was going to find for her. Taking with her the *Daily Telegraph*, a magazine and the chocolates she went up to her bedroom, partly undressed, and settled herself under the eiderdown, comfortably supported by pillows. The *Daily Telegraph*'s headlines were so off-putting that she threw the paper aside, and took up the magazine, popping a Marchpane Magic into her mouth as she did so. It was perfectly delicious: the thinnest shell of chocolate, and then rich creamy fudge before you got to the marzipan. Her hand reached out to the box again.

When Mrs Young was asked by her friends how in the world she put up with Mrs Vickers, she replied that there was always for and against. She had no doubt that the fors had it where her job at Lauriston was concerned. To begin with, the money was good, better than she let on to anyone except her husband. Then the work was nothing to grumble about: only the one lady, and no kiddies and animals messing the place up. Ten till twelve each morning suited her nicely, with nine till eleven on a Saturday to leave her time for her own place before the weekend.

On Saturday, 5 May, she arrived at the house just before nine to find that Mrs Vickers had forgotten to put up the catch of the front door for her. Using the latchkey entrusted to her she proceeded to let herself in.

'I'm here, Mrs Vickers,' she called out.

There was no answer. The doors of the downstairs rooms were open, and some of the windows, So Mrs Vickers was up and about. In the toilet, maybe, Mrs Young reflected, and not wanting to draw attention to it. She donned an overall and got out the hoover to run over the sitting-room. Not that it needed it every day, but the only way to keep the place nice was never to let things go.

She had almost finished when it struck her as a bit odd that Mrs Vickers still hadn't shown up. Most days she'd have been running round after you and talking the hind leg off a donkey. She couldn't have been taken bad, surely? Suddenly uneasy, Mrs Young switched off the hoover and went out into the hall.

'You all right. Mrs Vickers?' she called.

Once again there was no reply, and the house seemed uncannily quiet. With sudden decision Mrs Young ran up the stairs. There was no one in either the bathroom or the lavatory, and she knocked loudly on the closed door of Mrs Vickers' bedroom, her heart beating faster as she did so. On getting no answer for the third time she opened the door. She took a step towards the bed, and then froze. She had seen death before and could recognize it.

'Oh, my Gawd!' she whispered, backing out of the room, and steadying herself against the banisters at the top of the stairs. 'Oh, my Gawd! She must've 'ad a fit.'

As the morning wore on a small army of men occupied Lauriston. They appeared too large for its rather precious and immaculate rooms which echoed to their loud voices and heavy tread. In the road outside a crowd grew steadily, gazing at the house and the police cars.

Chief Inspector Dart of the Highcastle CID talked over the telephone to the Fulminster inspector who had contacted the Langs as Audrey Vickers' next-of-kin. Mr Lang, the inspector reported, had been at home, and seemed staggered by the news, saying that he supposed it must have been a heart attack. He had then been driven to the Technical College to break the news to his wife. She, too, had seemed very surprised, but neither of them had shown any signs of being distressed. As requested, enquiries had been made about Mrs Lang's job at the Tech. She was an assistant lecturer in chemistry.

Dart thanked Fulminster and rang off. He sat for a few moments digesting this information. He was pessimistic by nature, but allowed himself to register distinct interest. He had a retentive, if rather slow-moving mind, and had not failed to notice Mrs Young's slight hesitation when asked about deceased's next-of-kin.

Getting to his feet he went thoughtfully upstairs. Audrey Vickers' bedroom had a bizarre appearance, its furniture thrust at crazy angles to facilitate photography, and a series of white chalk circles on the carpet marking the positions of scattered chocolates and reading matter now removed. The still figure on the bed was covered by a sheet. Dr James Fosby, the pathologist, was standing with rolled-up sleeves washing his hands.

'I'm through,' he told Dart. 'Useful that the police surgeon happened to be her own doctor. I agree with him absolutely. It's cyanide, without a doubt. You can smell it, and there are all the text-book indications—colour, and what-have-you. It looks as though the stuff was in the chocolates. There are traces of chocolate in the mouth, and it's very fast-acting. Matter of a minute or so. How many had gone from the box?'

'Two. We've collected 'em all up, and fitted 'em into the slots in the packing material.'

'Two would be more than enough, assuming that the chap who doctored them knew the ropes. A lethal dose is only about enough to cover half of one of the old silver three-penny bits. Come on,' he added, throwing down the towel. 'I'm waiting for the thousand dollar question.'

Dart grinned.

'All right. What about it?'

'Death occurred not more than twenty-eight and not less than sixteen hours ago. That's as far as I'm ready to go at this stage. Any use to you? She'd hardly have been eating chocolates in the small hours, surely?'

'It could fit quite well; if the stuff was in the chocolates, that is. We've found the outside wrapping of a small parcel which the daily woman swears came by the midday post yesterday, and it fits the box perfectly. She also says Mrs Vickers was a rare one for sweets.'

Dr Fosby grunted as he struggled into his coat.

'Mortuary van here yet?'

'Just drawing up,' Dart replied from the window.

The police photographer emerged from the corner of the room and prepared for further activity during the removal of the body. This operation was conducted with meticulous care under the supervision of Dart and the pathologist. The latter then drove off ahead of the van to make arrangements for the post-mortem.

Dart watched the departures with a sense of relief, and

turned back into the house.

'Got that statement ready?' he asked, and took a typewritten sheet from his sergeant.

In the kitchen he found Mrs Young hunched passively at the table, her buxom arms resting on the buttercup-yellow formica, and an empty teacup in front of her.

'Sorry we've had to keep you waiting about like this, Mrs Young,' he told her.

'Reckon it can't be 'elped,' she replied philosophically.

Dart sat down facing her, and passed a typewritten sheet across the table.

'This is the very clear statement you made just now about what you did in the house yesterday morning and this morning. I only wish all the people we interview were as clear-headed as you are. I want you to read it over, and if you agree with it we'll ask you to put your name to it. All right?'

He watched her reading, her lips moving silently in the manner of one not too familiar with the printed word. Sensible reliable type, he thought with approval, and wondered how far she could be made to talk. As he waited he glanced round the room. Fitted kitchen in the luxury class, he decided. Vickers must have been pretty well-heeled. Who benefits? A niece doesn't automatically these days, even if she is next-of-kin . . .

'I'll sign,' Mrs Young told him.

'Fine,' he said, handing her his pen.

He waited while she inscribed her name slowly and carefully at the bottom of the typescript.

'Mr and Mrs Lang have been told of Mrs Vickers' death by the police at Fulminster,' he said, restoring the pen to his pocket. 'They're coming down this evening.'

Mrs Young looked startled.

'Will they be coming 'ere?'

'Not tonight, at any rate. You see, we don't yet know for certain the cause of Mrs Vickers' death, and there will have to be an enquiry. Until that's been made, we can't hand over the house.'

Dart decided that while she did not seem to have grasped the implications of what he had said, she looked relieved. He decided to bluff.

'Difficult when there are differences with relatives,' he remarked.

Mrs Young gave him a sharp look. Then, apparently accepting the omniscience of a high-up policeman, she nodded.

'Mind you, there weren't no differences before Mrs Lang went off and got married so sudden. Never said a word to Mrs Vickers till 'twas done. Seein' that she'd brought 'er up from a little 'un, and sent her to school and college, 'twas natural Mrs Vickers was upset.'

'Quite natural,' Dart agreed. 'I suppose Mrs Lang was afraid her aunt wouldn't approve of the bridegroom?'

'No more she did. 'E 'adn't got no proper job—just tryin' to write books. Mrs Lang didn't act proper to her auntie over it, not to my way of thinkin'. But mind you, Mrs Vickers 'ung on to 'er like a limpet, an' young people'll go their own way sooner or later these days, an' that's a fac', whether you likes it or not.'

'When did the Langs get married?'

'Last August, 'twas, soon as Mrs Lang had got her degree up to Oxford. They wanted 'er to stay on an' do summat else, but she went off with 'im instead.'

'Have the Langs been on visiting terms with Mrs Vickers since?'

'Not visitin', they 'aven't. But they've all been on a cruise together. Mrs Vickers paid. They only got back Tuesday.'

'That looks as if the quarrel had been made up, doesn't it?' said Dart, with the feeling of a promising lead petering out.

To his surprise a sudden cautious expression came into Mrs Young's face.

'Mr and Mrs Lang'll be able to tell you more about that than what I can,' she replied after a noticeable pause.

'Of course they will,' Dart agreed pleasantly. 'Now, just one more question before you go. Do you know the name of Mrs Vickers' solicitor?'

Mrs Young's cautious expression remained.

'That'll be Mr Partridge, over to Highcastle,' she said reluctantly.

Judging that it would be useless to press his enquiries further, Dart let her go, after warning her that she would be required to give evidence at the inquest.

Partridge, Webster and Partridge of Monday Street, he thought, making for Audrey Vickers' desk. He found that 'Mr P' was scrawled against ten am for the previous day. Mrs Young obviously knew something about that appointment, and also about developments on the cruise, and it wasn't difficult to put two and two together. Unconscious loyalty to her late employer coming to the surface, he wondered briefly, or just reluctance to get mixed up with the cops?

Dart pulled himself up. He was beginning to speculate, and it wouldn't do at this stage. He decided that he disliked the case. Murder by what you might call remote control had never come his way before. Why, it could be tied up with things happening on that cruise hundreds of miles away. Not his cup of tea at all. He liked nice tangible clues lending themselves to investigation on the spot by himself and his chaps.

Feeling gloomy, he opened the drawers of the desk one after another. One thing, deceased seemed to have been a businesslike type, with her affairs in good order. All these papers would have to be gone through, but for the moment he'd have the place locked up with a man on guard, go back to Highcastle to report to the Chief Constable and wait for the outcome of the postmortem. Then come back later to interview the Langs.

Objects for immediate removal and investigation were set out on the table in the dining-room, in neatly labelled plastic bags. Dart ran his eye over the soiled crockery and cutlery which Mrs Vickers had stacked in the dishwasher after her lunch on the previous day, the remains of a cold chicken, a half-empty carton of some sort of salad and various other items taken from the refrigerator. It seemed quite impossible that any of these latter could have been the vehicle of the cyanide, but you couldn't be too careful in a murder case. He scrutinized the brown paper wrapping with tatty bits of sellotape adhering to it, and wondered if the handwriting experts would ever be able to make anything of the featureless block capitals of the address.

'Get all this junk on board, and the place properly secured,' he said to his sergeant. 'I'll ring the local station about a relief for the chap they posted outside.'

It was as he crossed the hall that something small and bright on the carpet caught his eye. Further investigation showed that it was a scrap of Sellotape, and the fragment of brown paper sticking to it seemed identical with the wrapping he had just been looking at. Dart stood frowning for a moment, his mind labouring with an idea. In her statement Mrs Young had said that she had picked up the midday post and put it on the chest in the hall. It seemed a reasonable deduction that Mrs Vickers, coming in from her trip to Highcastle, might have stood in front of the chest opening her mail, and had a bit of bother getting the wrapping off the parcel. He leant forward and peered behind the chest.

'Here, come and lend a hand, one of you,' he called. 'I want to see what's dropped down behind this contraption.'

A minute later he was cautiously lifting a printed slip of paper by its edges. 'With the compliments of Odyssey Tours Ltd,' he read. Above the word was a rum looking boat. He sniffed cautiously, and recognized an unmistakable smell of chocolate.

That ruddy cruise, he thought. This must be phoney, though. Even if they really handed out chocolates to passengers as an advert, they'd do it on the last night of the trip, surely? That label, too ... Hand-printed in ink, not typed, as anything from the office would be. The office'll be shut for the weekend by now ...

With extreme care Dart transferred the compliments slip and the fragment of Sellotape to clean envelopes from his case, sealing and labelling them. He then rang the Redbay police station about a relief for the constable posted at the gate, and after a final glance round went out of the house slamming the front door behind him and testing it carefully.

During the drive back to Highcastle the prospect of working on the case filled him with gloom. Unless it could be established that the niece and her husband had done the old girl for her money, there'd be no end to it. Why, the people who could have got hold of those slips and knew Vickers had just been on a cruise must run into hundreds. Fancy trying to follow 'em up, and find out which of 'em had a link with her. A Yard job, if ever there was one. What would the CC think?

Only recently promoted to his Chief-Inspectorship, Dart found that he did not at all relish the idea of being patronized by some blighter down from the Yard. Too much to hope that they'd get another bloke like Pollard, who'd been sent along over the Affacombe business ...

On his arrival at headquarters he collided with Colonel Brand, the Chief Constable, who was coming out of the main entrance.

'Very sorry, sir,' he exclaimed apologetically.

'Glad you're back. We've got another murder on our hands.'

Dart opened his eyes wide.

'Yes,' Colonel Brand continued. 'Chap with a knife in his back, found by kids behind a bush in the recreation ground. I was just going along myself, but now you've turned up I'd better hear about this Redbay show, if you can make it snappy.'

Inside, Dart made a competent statement of bare facts.

The Chief Constable, an outdoor type whose face could have been carved out of seasoned teak, listened without comment.

'The report on that fire at Roccombe has come in,' he said with apparent irrelevance when Dart had finished talking. 'It's arson, without the slightest doubt, the forensic chaps say. So that means a manslaughter charge, as a body was found in the rubble. What about it? Can we possibly carry all three jobs?'

'Don't see how we can sir, on our present strength, do you? For one thing, this Redbay affair doesn't look like a local job to me. Not a straightforward one, anyway.'

'Meaning that's the one you'd suggest pushing off on to the Yard?'

'That's the one, certainly, sir,' Dart replied, conscious of an inner surge of hope.

Colonel Brand sat in silent meditation.

'I'm inclined to agree,' he said at last. 'After all, we've done quite a bit of work on that fire already—not that there's much to show for it yet. And this knifing's almost certainly one of the local thugs. I think I'd better get on to the Yard right away. Ask for Pollard again, don't you think? He knows our set-up here, and it'll save no end of time.'

'Not much chance of a stroke of luck like that,' Dart observed gloomily.

'The trouble with you is that you're such a ruddy pessimist,' Colonel Brand remarked amicably, reaching for the telephone receiver.

Returning to his own room Dart found the analyst's report on the chocolates awaiting him. He was engrossed in it when a head came round the door.

'Detective-Superintendent Pollard will arrive at nine-thirty on the London train,' his Chief Constable informed him triumphantly.

FOUR

By leaving the sitting-room door wide open Jane Pollard could keep an eye on the increasingly mobile twins while taking a telephone call from her husband at New Scotland Yard. She heard the familiar news of his immediate departure from London with a resigned groan.

'Where is it this time?' she asked.

'Highcastle,' Detective-Superintendent Tom Pollard told her.

'*Highcastle*? How extraordinary!'

'Not in the least extraordinary. Naturally they asked for me after last time.'

'On the devil you know principle, I suppose? Well, anyway, it's nearer than Newcastle. Or Boscastle. Train or car?'

'Train, to save time.'

'Good. Much less lethal. Tom! Rose is up!'

'Up where?'

'On her two feet for the first time, idiot! She hoicked herself up holding on to your chair. Now she's just collapsed on to her bottom again, looking puzzled. Andrew's giving her a disapproving stare, like a shop steward who's spotted an over-enthusiastic worker.'

'Hell!' exclaimed Pollard disgustedly. 'Just when I've got to go off. Right now—Toye's hovering. If I don't ring you by eleven, I'll ring early tomorrow . . .'

Some hours later three men of diverse physical type sat in Chief-Inspector Dart's room at the Highcastle police headquarters. Dart, a very tall man, dark and with a sombre hatchet face, was at his desk, the newly-inaugurated file of the Vickers case open in front of him as he talked. Detective-Superintendent Pollard, tall, fair and loose-limbed, appeared relaxed as he listened with his long legs crossed and arms folded. On his left his sergeant, Gregory Toye, who only just achieved regulation height, was pale and serious. Large horn-rimmed spectacles enhanced the inscrutability of his expression.

'Well, that's about the size of it up to now,' Dart concluded, shutting the file and pushing it across his desk.

'Thanks,' said Pollard. 'You couldn't have set it out more clearly.'

Toye, from his experience of working with Pollard, correctly detected a note of reserve. Listening to Dart, the latter had reflected that while the Chief-Inspector had certainly mellowed since their previous collaboration, he was still the same thorough methodical chap uninterested in people as human beings. The case was meticulously documented up to date, but Mrs Audrey Vickers remained a well-heeled widow of fifty-five. Only an addiction to sweets and possessiveness towards her niece hinted at her personality.

He looked at his watch.

'It's too late to go over to Redbay and see the Langs tonight,' he said. 'Anyway, there's a lot in this file for us to digest first. Where are they putting up?'

'Vicarage,' replied Dart. 'Seems Mrs Vickers was in with the church, and when the news got round the vicar turned up at the station and asked if he could do anything to help the Langs.'

'They'd better come along to the station, I think. Most vicarages are public places within the meaning of the act these days. Can whoever's in charge get on to them? Say ten o'clock, so that we can take a look at the house first.'

'Sure,' Dart said. 'I'll ring Inspector Morris.'

'Well, if you'll do that, we'll clear off now. You've enough on your plate without us hanging around. Are we at the same pub as last time?'

'Yes.' Dart told them, 'the Southgate. Turn left when you go out of here.'

'I remember. Comfortable, and decent grub.'

'If you ask me,' Dart said, escorting them to the door, 'there's more than one pointer to that young couple.'

The Southgate was barely three minutes' walk from police headquarters, and in a short space of time Pollard and Toye had established themselves, collected a couple of tankards of beer and retreated to the far depths of a deserted lounge.

'Now we can mop all this up in peace and quiet,' Pollard remarked opening the file and flicking over its contents. 'Preliminary routine procedure ... photographs ... dabs ... daily woman's statement ... pathologist's report ... analyst's report ... Fulminster ... Odyssey Tours ... the lot.'

For some time there was silence as the two men read steadily through the paperwork on the case assembled by Dart.

'What's your first reaction?' Pollard asked at last, throwing down the report of the post-mortem and sprawling back in his chair.

'Wicked recklessness,' Toye replied indignantly. 'A lethal dose of cyanide in every one of those chocolates. Could have polished off half a dozen people.'

'I'm not sure it was all that reckless,' Pollard said meditatively. 'Whoever sent them knew quite a bit about Mrs Vickers and her way of life. That she was a compulsive sweet-guzzler, for instance, and almost certainly that she lived alone. The sender was someone with access to cyanide, of course, and knowledge of its effects. Its rapid action would cut out a good deal of third-party risk where someone living alone was concerned.'

'Somebody pretty neat-fingered, too,' suggested Toye. 'All that in the analyst's report about taking a bit out of each chocolate with a thing like a minute apple corer, and then standing the finished product on a bit of foil over low heat to get the mark smeared over. What does the stuff look like?'

'Damp cooking salt,' Pollard told him. 'And the lethal dose is a tiny pinch. There's a surprising lot of it around, too—quite legally. On farms for getting rid of wasps' nests, and in light engineering works, and in labs, of course.'

Toye blinked behind his spectacles.

'What price Inspector Dart's pointers, sir? Mrs Lang teaching chemistry at a tech, with good labs, I don't doubt. You'd have to be quite handy for doing experiments, wouldn't you?'

'All very true. But whoever sent those chocolates had to be able to get hold of them in the first place, and post them in London on Thursday. The Langs' movements will have to be gone into, of course, and then there's the question of motive. The row over the marriage obviously didn't lead to a final break because of all three of them going on this cruise. At the moment the only evidence we've got that there was another bust-up during the trip is Dart's impression that the daily woman was being cagey on the subject, and also about the Vickers' rather suggestive visit to her solicitor on Friday morning. He's one of our high priorities, incidentally. How about some more beer?'

As Toye set off for the bar Pollard began to jot down notes under the headings 'Langs: Facts' and 'Langs: Enquiries'. He then took another slip of paper from the supply he always carried with him when on a case, and headed it 'Audrey Vickers'. At this point Toye reappeared, walking with a full tankard in each hand and intense concentration.

'Thanks,' said Pollard. 'Cheers.' He took a long refreshing

pull and settled himself comfortably in his chair. 'Now, Vickers. We know practically nothing about her, and to dear old Dart she's just something that's got to be tidied up. What's her background, past and present? Where did all her money come from? What sort of life does she lead in Redbay, apart from going to church? Likely sources of information: Langs (with some reservations at the moment), the daily woman, the doctor, the solicitor, the vicar,' he went on, scribbling as he talked.

'Local force?' queried Toye.

'Could be useful,' agreed Pollard, 'even in these days of panda cars instead of the chap on the beat. Then Records. Her dabs will be checked automatically, but I want her birth, marriage, husband's death, etc, all looked up.'

'What about the Langs, sir?'

'We'll check up on them, too. It has just occurred to me that Mrs Vickers might have suddenly discovered that they weren't legally married, and it was that which blew things sky-high. We'll take their dabs tomorrow. In the meantime you can ring the Yard and get the enquiries in train, while I stick down a few more points. Then we'll turn in. Tomorrow looks like being quite a day.'

'It looks as though we'll be clocking up the mileage today,' Pollard told Jane, ringing her from his room at the Southgate early on Sunday, and using their motoring code. 'I wouldn't know what driving conditions'll be like down here ... What? ... No, I'm just going down to breakfast now ... No, not a hope of getting back before tomorrow night, from what I can see at the moment ... Has Rose put on a repeat performance ...?'

Cheered by the contact with his home he spurned the lift, ran down three flights of stairs and overtook Toye on the way to the dining-room. Over bacon and eggs they drew up a provisional timetable for the day ahead, and were round at police headquarters by eight-thirty. Dart, they learnt, had already gone out in connection with the stabbing in the recreation ground, but had left Pollard a note saying that the inquest on Mrs Vickers would be open at Redbay at two-thirty pm on the following day, and that the dabs on the chocolate box were worth looking at.

Detective-Constable Bragg, the young photographic expert of the Highcastle CID, impressed Pollard favourably. Although shy at finding himself unsupported in exalted company, he showed at the same time the confidence of an efficient technician. The box of Marchpane Magic was produced, together with its wrappings and a series of blown-up photographs of fingerprints.

'You wouldn't have thought they'd have used a smooth brown paper like this to go outside the parcel,' he said. 'It takes prints quite well. These are deceased's, where she gripped with her left hand when she was opening the package. Then one of this other lot is clear enough to identify with the daily woman's, when she picked it up. I reckon she was a bit hot and sweaty.'

'I expect she was, after her morning stint of housework on a warm day,' Pollard replied. 'What do you make of these smudges, Bragg?'

'Nothing that'll stand up, sir, beyond the fact that somebody who handled the parcel wore gloves. Here, do you see?'

'Yes,' Pollard said, after a careful scrutiny. 'Hardly likely that the sorters or the postman did, is it?'

The box itself was enclosed in a cellophane wrapping. It fitted tightly, and Audrey Vickers had only partly torn it open. Here again, her own prints were clearly impressed, together with recognizable gloved prints. These were smallish, and Bragg suggested that they could have been made by a woman. It was however, two further prints which made Pollard exclaim in surprise.

'Rum, isn't it, sir?' Bragg said with satisfaction. 'Just the thumb and first finger of a little kiddy's right hand on this one corner of the packet. Looks as though he'd tried to pull it out of somewhere.'

Pollard agreed, thinking of the exploratory activities of the twins.

'At the moment,' he said, 'it just doesn't add up, but it could turn out a top lead, you know. You've done a jolly good job of work on these dabs, and I shall be telling Inspector Dart about it. Well, I suppose we'd better be pushing off to Redbay now, Sergeant Toye. Where's this car you people are laying on for us?'

'Out this way, sir,' replied Constable Bragg, slightly pink with gratification. He led the way to a side door giving on to the car park.

It was a perfect May morning, golden and palest blue, and at this early hour still enfolded in sabbath peace. A few miles out of Highcastle they branched off from the main road, and were soon running between high hedges frothing with young green.

'Look at those primroses!' Pollard exclaimed. 'And that gorse!' He hastily let down the window. 'Can't you smell it? Coconut buns just out of the oven.' He sniffed vigorously. 'When you think of the stink of petrol in London . . .'

Toye, cautiously overtaking a milk-lorry, agreed that on a day like this the country was a bit of all right.

Pollard reluctantly brought his thoughts back from the landscape to his case. Those small glove prints. Were they another pointer to the niece? He couldn't be too careful to approach the Lang interview with an absolutely open mind.

He went on to consider the implications of a possible elimination of the Langs. It would mean that Audrey Vickers had had an enemy prepared to take the risk of murdering her: an unusual situation, to say the least of it, for a woman in late middle-age leading to an uneventful life in a small seaside resort. Surely someone in her circle would know about an antagonism on this scale? The Langs themselves, for instance, or some local friend, or perhaps her solicitor . . .

Pollard roused himself to answer a query from Toye.

'Yes, the station first. Better just to drop in before we go along to the house.'

The Redbay police station was in the charge of Inspector Morris, a quiet man rather slow of speech, who nevertheless impressed Pollard favourably. He reported that the Langs had arrived at the Vicarage much later than expected the night before, owing to engine trouble as they drove down. They would be along at ten o'clock as the Superintendent had asked.

'Properly het up, Mrs Lang,' Inspector Morris said. 'Said she was being kept in the dark about her auntie, and what exactly had happened? I stalled, and handed out the usual about an enquiry into the cause of death when the doctor couldn't give a certificate, and how Highcastle was conducting this one. It was before Inspector Dart rang to say you were taking over, sir. She carried on about red tape, and then she asked point-blank if Mrs Vickers had taken her own life. I said I'd no information to give her, and that an officer from Highcastle would tell her all she wanted to know this morning.'

'How did the question about Mrs Vickers taking her own life strike you?' Pollard asked. 'Genuine?'

Inspector Morris looked at him shrewdly.

'Well, yes, it did. Quite genuine, for all that she was rattled.'

'Did you know Mrs Vickers?'

'Not to say know her. I didn't. I knew her by sight. One of those jerky hurried walkers, she was, going along with her head poking forward and looking tensed up. She'd ring with a complaint now and again—parking outside her gate mostly. Excitable type who'd talk the hind leg off a donkey. There's never been anything outstanding about her. She never took a big part locally, but you'd see her around with others of her sort. Plenty in the kitty, I'd say.'

'Thanks,' said Pollard. 'This sort of stuff from you local chaps is a great help. You've never heard of her having a serious row or a feud with anybody round here?'

'Nothing in that way, sir. I wouldn't say she was popular, but I've never heard of anything of that sort.'

'What's Mrs Lang like?'

'She's a little bit of a thing with reddish hair. Mrs Vickers brought her up from all accounts. She's been away a lot—boarding-school, and then college. Said to be very clever, and there was a piece in the local paper last summer about her degree at Oxford, I think it was. I heard tell there'd been a bust-up with Mrs Vickers about the marriage, and come to think of it, Mrs Lang hasn't shown up in these parts lately.'

Pollard thanked him again.

'I'd like to run up for a quick look at the house,' he said. 'We'll be back by ten.'

Lauriston, Audrey Vickers' house, was in a quiet road in the older, residential part of Redbay. It was of moderate size, double-fronted and with big bay windows overlooking a trim garden gay with flowering trees and a splendid show of tulips. As Pollard and Toye arrived a constable emerged from the summer-house. No one, he said, had turned up since he took over at seven that morning, except a paper boy and the milkman. He produced a key and let the Yard men into the house.

It was stale and frowsty inside. The place hadn't had a window open since Dart and his lot were here yesterday, Pollard thought, walking into the main sitting-room on the left of the front door. Behind some superficial disorder he recognized decoration and furnishings in rather old-fashioned good taste. Among the pictures were a couple of portraits in oils which he put down as eighteenth or early nineteenth century, some amatuer water colours in Victorian gilt frames and one or two modern landscapes. There was a fine Chippendale table, and other extremely pleasing pieces, and a display of Rockingham china in a cabinet. All this could have been picked up in sale-rooms and antique shops, but it somehow looked like family stuff, and suggested a stable and prosperous background. There was a complete absence of clutter, and Pollard was reminded of his maiden aunt's elegant little cottage, except that here there were chairs representing the last word in luxurious modern comfort. As he went quickly through the rest of the house he found the same emphasis on comfort everywhere. The carpets stretched from wall to wall, and were soft and deep. Mattresses were covered with brocade, and of a positively bloated thickness. The bathroom and kitchen were lavishly equipped with every possible gadget. There was central heating and double glazing. His Aunt Isabel would think it all rather vulgar, if not sinfully self-indulgent, but it all helped him to build up a picture of Audrey Vickers. She had certainly been at pains to cushion herself with a hefty layer of material well-being. Against what, he wondered? The bleakness of an early widowhood?

A rapid inspection of cupboards and drawers led him to Dart's conclusion. Audrey Vickers had kept her affairs on an orderly footing.

'It shouldn't take long to go through this lot,' he said to Toye, as they stood in front of a handsome bureau-bookcase. 'If there's time after seeing the Langs, and I can contact the solicitor, I think I'll cut back to Highcastle while you start having a bash here. She doesn't seem to have kept letters, but we might come on something useful.'

Toye subjected the room to a contemplative gaze.

'Lush, but a bit chilly,' he pronounced at last. 'Impersonal, somehow.'

'Have you noticed there isn't a photograph in the place?' Pollard asked. 'Nothing of the late Mr Vickers, or of the niece she's brought up from a kid. Odd, isn't it? Here, I must be going.'

Pollard's immediate impression of Drusilla Lang was that she was trying to conceal acute unhappiness under a show of aggressiveness. Telling Inspector Morris that he would rather introduce himself, he had walked into the small room where she was waiting with her husband, Toye following him.

'Good morning,' he said. 'I'm Superintendent Pollard of the

CID, and this is Sergeant Toye. You are Mr and Mrs Lang, I understand, and Mrs Lang is the late Mrs Vickers' niece? I'm afraid her death must have been a great shock to you. May I express my sympathy?'

'I'd far rather you gave me some information,' Drusilla Lang replied truculently. 'I haven't been able to get a word of sense out of the local police. What happened to my aunt?'

She stood confronting him, small and slight in a beige linen suit with a diminutive mini-skirt, her long tawny hair making her look like a child until the observer's eyes moved to her intelligent face and determined chin. Her husband appeared large and even massive by comparison, although only of average height. Intelligent too, Pollard registered, although quite a different type. He stood close to his wife, and gave the impression of being anxious about what she might say or do.

'Shall we sit down?' Pollard suggested.

The Langs subsided on to two upright chairs on the far side of the table, facing him. Toye effaced himself somewhere in the background.

'Naturally you're entitled to know what has happened to your aunt, Mrs Lang,' Pollard told her. 'You're Mrs Vickers' next-of-kin, aren't you?'

'Yes,' she replied impatiently. 'I believe she had some distant cousins up north somewhere, but she had lost touch with them.'

'At about a quarter-past nine yesterday morning,' Pollard stated, 'Mrs Vickers was found dead by her daily woman, a Mrs Young. She was lying on her bed, and appeared to have gone there to rest after her lunch on Friday. There has been a post-mortem examination, and the estimated time of death bears out this theory. Mrs Young rang for Dr Cross, who came round immediately. He found himself unable to give a death certificate, and notified Inspector Morris here. The Inspector in his turn reported the matter to his superiors at Highcastle, and Chief-Inspector Dart of the Highcastle CID took over the enquiry.'

As he talked, Pollard watched the Langs closely. Keith was frowning as if with intense concentration. An angry flush spread over Drusilla's face.

'Then why isn't he here, if he's supposed to be in charge?' she demanded indignantly. 'I should have thought he'd have come over to see me out of common decency. Or perhaps the police haven't time for that sort of thing. Who are you, anyway?'

'Sergeant Toye and I are members of the Criminal Investigation Department of New Scotland Yard, Mrs Lang. The Chief Constable has asked the Yard to take over from Highcastle.'

There was an electric silence. Either they're consummate actors, Pollard thought, studying the stupefaction of the two faces in front of him, or they just haven't a clue...

'But what the hell's the idea?' Keith broke out unexpectedly. 'It seems pretty obvious that Mrs Vickers killed herself, but suicide's not a crime now.'

'I must tell you both that there is no question of suicide, nor of an accident in the ordinary sense of the word. We are treating the case as one of murder, Mr Lang.'

'But it's—it's simply preposterous,' Drusilla exclaimed, bringing her hand down on the table. 'There's some absurd mistake!'

'Briefly, the facts are these,' Pollard said, ignoring this remark. 'A small parcel addressed to Mrs Vickers arrived at Lauriston by the second delivery on Friday. This is vouched for by Mrs Young. It contained half a pound of chocolates. After her lunch, when she had gone to her bedroom to rest, Mrs Vickers ate two of these chocolates, and the post-mortem has established that she died from a lethal dose of cyanide. Analysis of the remaining chocolates has found a lethal dose of cyanide in each one. With the box was a compliments slip from Odyssey Tours Limited. We are contacting the firm, of course, but I think we may rule out any possibility of the chocolates having been sent out from their office.'

Drusilla had gone very white. She made an involuntary movement towards her husband, who shifted his chair closer to hers.

'Now that you know the facts,' Pollard went on, with a more official note in his voice, 'you'll both realize, I'm sure, that we have to ask everyone closely connected with Mrs Vickers a lot of what may seem very tiresome questions. But before I begin, I have to remind you that you are not obliged to answer any of them, and that your solicitor may be present if you wish.'

He thought the pair looked young and frightened. Then Drusilla flared out at him.

'I suppose you've already decided that I did it, to get her money? Well, let me tell you there wasn't any as far as I was concerned. Aunt Audrey had cut me out of her will.'

Keith grabbed her arm roughly.

'For God's sake don't talk such bloody rot,' he adjured her

49

angrily. 'The chap's got to do his job.'

'Forcibly put, but all too true,' Pollard remarked.

The tactic worked. Drusilla shook back her hair, mumbling something shamefacedly.

'... Bit of a shock. What is it, you want to know?'

'Let's begin at the beginning,' Pollard suggested. 'You were left an orphan, weren't you, and Mrs Vickers brought you up?'

'Yes. Both my parents were killed in a plane crash when I was three. There wasn't a penny—they'd been living it up—and Aunt Audrey took me on. She was a well-off widow, and—well —gave me everything. Top school, holidays abroad, Oxford— the lot.'

'What went wrong, then, since you say she's cut you out of her will?'

Drusilla indicated her husband.

'It was bound to happen. Aunt Audrey was a pathetic frustrated person, and madly possessive. She just lived on me—emotionally, I mean. I was hopelessly immature when I went to Oxford, but I soon came to. I'd just realized that I'd have to make a breakaway when I met Keith, you see. College had offered me a research studentship—I got a first, actually—but instead we went off and got married without telling anyone. I honestly thought it was better for everyone to have the row with Aunt Audrey afterwards.'

'Did your marriage lead to a complete break?'

'Not at first. She even wanted to make me an allowance, but there were strings, so I wouldn't take it.'

'Strings relating to me,' Keith put in. 'I haven't a nine-till-five job, you see. I write—or try to. Mrs Vickers disapproved.'

'Keith's going to make the grade,' Drusilla said with passionate conviction in her voice. 'Thrale's have just taken his first novel, and think a lot of it. I've got a part-time teaching job at the Fulminster Tech so that we can make out till he gets going. We were getting along perfectly well until we both went down with flu rather badly in January. Keith sprang pneumonia, and was very ill. I think Aunt Audrey really tried to be decent at this point. She offered to take us both on a Mediterranean cruise in April, to get fit again. Keith wasn't keen, but I thought it would do him good, and insisted on going. And,' she paused, fumbling for words, 'I am—was—awfully sorry for her, you know. And grateful for all she'd done. I knew she'd be difficult on the trip, but we were someone for her to go with. You know.'

'I see,' said Pollard.

By dint of further questions he formed the opinion that Audrey Vickers had been unreasonably demanding on the cruise, but the Langs had contrived to enjoy themselves within limits until there was a major blow-up almost at the end.

At this point he thought that the Langs became ill at ease. Pressed to explain how the trouble had arisen, they gave an unconvincing account of Audrey Vickers' sudden indisposition on the Acropolis, her insistence on their returning with her to the ship, and their walk-out for the rest of the day in order to see something of Athens. On their return, Drusilla told him, her aunt had been in an uncontrollable rage, and said such unforgivable things that she had decided then and there that they'd reached the point of no return. For the rest of the cruise they had barely spoken, and had parted at Heathrow with no attempt at reconciliation from either side.

'And there has been no contact between you since?' Pollard asked.

'None,' Drusilla replied with finality.

'As a matter of routine I must ask you both how you spent your time after parting from Mrs Vickers at Heathrow.'

Pollard was aware that Keith had begun to look at him fixedly.

'Aunt Audrey didn't offer us a lift in her taxi to Waterloo,' Drusilla said. 'In any case we'd decided to go down to Fulminster by a later train to keep clear of her. We went into London by bus, and went to the British Museum to see the Elgin Marbles. Then we had some tea, and got buses to Waterloo, and caught the five-thirty down.'

'And what about the following days?'

'Term began on Wednesday. I was at the Tech all day, and stayed late to do things in the lab. And Thursday. Wednesday, Thursday and Friday are my days there.'

'I was in the flat all Wednesday, except for going out to get some food and things,' Keith said steadily. 'On Thursday I went up to London to see Thrale's about my novel. There was a letter waiting when we got back saying they'd like to see me on Thursday.'

There was a perceptible pause. Toye turned over a page in his notebook.

'Mrs Lang,' Pollard asked, 'Mrs Vickers only got back to her home here on Tuesday afternoon or evening. If, as you say, you

51

had no contact with her after you parted in London, how did you know that she had cut you out of her will?'

Drusilla looked taken aback, but met his eyes quite frankly.

'I don't know in the sense of knowing some demonstrable scientific fact,' she admitted. 'But I'm morally certain. She told me that the moment she got home she was going to ring her solicitor in Highcastle for an appointment the next day, and make a new will there and then, and wasn't leaving me a penny. She was the kind of person who always rushed off and did things at once, even if she wasn't in a flaming rage, wasn't she, Keith?'

He nodded assent.

Pollard took a small booklet from his brief case.

'Naturally the Odyssey Tours compliments slip with the chocolates doesn't prove that there is any connection between the cruise and your aunt's death,' he said, 'but I'd like to run through the passenger list with you both. Try to remember if Mrs Vickers seemed to be seeing much of anybody.'

'She didn't. People sheered off her,' Drusilla said bluntly. 'She talked a lot. Mostly about herself, and I'm quite sure about us, and how ghastly we were to her.'

'All the same, we'll have a bash,' Pollard insisted. 'Stop me if you do remember anything.'

He read the list aloud, pausing at intervals to tick the names of their table companions and those of one or two other people with whom Audrey Vickers had attempted to fraternize.

'Strode, Mrs Olivia,' he read, and stopped abruptly.

'She was awfully nice,' Drusilla remarked with warmth. 'She was around that morning on the Acropolis, and even offered to take Aunt Audrey back to the ship, so that we could stay up there, but it was no go. Aunt Audrey was beastly rude to her, actually.'

'Was Mrs Strode shortish, and rather plump? About sixty?'

'Yes, she was. Do you know her?'

'I think I do.' He ticked the name and went on with the list.

'I suppose there'll be an inquest?' Keith asked, when he had finished.

'I was coming to that,' Pollard said. 'It will be opened here at two-thirty tomorrow afternoon, simply to establish Mrs Vickers' identity, so that the coroner can issue the burial certificate. The inquest will be adjourned at once, probably for a fortnight, so that further enquiries can be made. I suggest that you or Mrs

Lang contact Mrs Vickers' solicitor. He will undoubtedly come over, and can tell you if she has left any wishes about her funeral. You will be staying for it of course?'

'Yes,' said Drusilla decisively. 'Then we can go home, I suppose?'

'Certainly. Only let the police know if you go away from home, in case we want to contact you. I needn't keep you any longer now.'

As he watched them go out of the room they struck him again as young and defenceless. Then his misgivings returned.

'What do you make of all that?' he asked Toye.

Toye looked up from screwing the top on to his pen.

'You'd hardly think those two had done it, would you? But after all, it's facts that tell, and there's a proper build-up, isn't there?'

'There is,' Pollard agreed, sitting on the edge of the table with his hands in his trouser pockets. 'Let's recap. They could have gone to the Honeydew shop and bought the chocolates on Tuesday afternoon. Mrs Lang could have brought cyanide back from the labs at the Tech on Wednesday evening. There was all night for doctoring the chocolates and packing 'em up, and on Thursday Lang goes up to London on perfectly legitimate business. It's as simple as that.'

'What's getting you, sir?' asked Toye.

Pollard frowned, balancing the heel of his right shoe on the toe of the left.

'It's so damned obvious,' he said at last, 'and they're anything but fools, Lang especially. As you'll have noticed, he's got there, and realizes that they're potentially in a spot. The girl may have a higher IQ, but she's emotionally immature, and so steamed up at the moment that she doesn't seem to see what it's all adding up to. Unless she's a first-class actress, that is . . . Of course, as far as the obviousness goes, it could be a double bluff. Then there's the question of motive. The money's one's first reaction. But if Vickers was the sort to dash into action the moment she'd made up her mind about something, the Langs were a bit leisurely, don't you think? And honestly, Toye, do you see those two committing murder for the sake of revenge, because I can't? Even if the girl felt like it because of the things Vickers has said about her husband, she couldn't have brought it off without his help because of posting the parcel in London on Thursday.'

'We've only her word for where she was all Thursday,' Toye objected.

'I'll grant you that, and we'll have to do some checking up in Fulminster, but she'd never be such a fool as to lie about being at the Tech. It could be disproved in a moment... Well, as I said just now, the next step's to see if I can get hold of this Partridge chap today. I expect he's playing golf or sailing, the lucky devil.'

Abandoning his balancing act, Pollard went in search of a telephone.

FIVE

It transpired that Mr Edward Partridge, solicitor to the late Audrey Vickers, was neither golfing nor sailing, but mowing the lawn of his house in Marton, a village between Redbay and Highcastle. Over the telephone he sounded puffed, and suggested that Pollard should call in with an alacrity which implied that a break would be welcome.

Pollard cast an envious eye on the house as he drew up on the gravel sweep outside the front door. Two, or possibly three cottages had been amalgamated to form a long low building, pink-washed and newly thatched, with fascinating straw topknots on the ridge of the roof. The garden was beautifully kept, and the scent of wallflowers, lilac and cut grass filled the air. A large electric mower had been abandoned in the middle of the lawn. As he got out of the car Mr Partridge emerged from the house, bearing the signs of a hasty toilet. His large face was flushed from manual labour under the hot sun.

'Superintendent Pollard? How d'ye do? Come along and have a spot of something, won't you? It's cooler inside.'

'I'm sorry to break in on your sabbath,' Pollard said, shaking hands, 'but you know what times means on a job like this.'

'Sabbath be blowed,' Mr Partridge grumbled, leading the way across the hall. 'Call it a day of rest! This damn grass is getting me down. Grows like wildfire. The chap who said the Greeks got where they did because they hadn't any grass to cope with had got something. In here. We shan't be disturbed.'

Pollard followed him into a comfortably furnished study.

54

'Sit down,' said his host, indicating large leather-covered armchairs. 'What'll you drink?'

When the cans of beer, tankards, cigarettes and tobacco jar had been collected, he lowered his considerable bulk into one of the chairs and eyed Pollard.

'Well, Superintendent, what can I do for you?'

'To begin with,' Pollard replied, 'I want you to tell me what sort of a person your late client was. Build her up in the round, so to speak. You've known her for some time, I take it?'

'Not all that long. Roughly ten years.'

'Is that ever since she settled in Redbay?'

'No. She'd lived there for about seventeen years. Originally she employed another local solicitor, and a very good chap he was, too, but she fell out with him and transferred her business to us.'

'Rows and drastic steps seem to have been characteristic of the lady,' Pollard remarked. 'To save time, I'd better explain that I've seen Mrs Lang, and had her back history and the reactions of Mrs Vickers to her marriage.'

Mr Partridge took a little time over lighting his pipe and getting it to draw to his satisfaction.

'My relationship with Mrs Vickers was purely professional,' he said. 'As a client she certainly wasn't easy, although a sensible woman in some ways—over money matters, for instance. The trouble was in herself. In the modern jargon she suffered from a sense of insecurity, perhaps as the result of her early widowhood. I don't know the details, but I understand that she married in the first months of the war, and that her husband was killed shortly afterwards. At all events, she was perpetually on the defensive, and on the lookout for threats to her well-being and security. She'd work herself into a frenzy about something, and want to take legal action. For instance, on one occasion she heard a rumour that the road she lived in was going to be widened by a slice being taken off the gardens. She rushed in to see me in a frantic state, wanting to apply for an injunction against the County Council. There wasn't a grain of truth in it.'

'We're naturally very interested in any personal enmities that she had aroused,' Pollard remarked.

'Surprisingly, perhaps, in the light of what I've just said, I don't think I can help you there,' Mr Partridge replied. 'She had various rows with her neighbours about parking and bonfires and what-have-you, and used to turn up gunning for some-body at intervals, but I always managed to head her off taking whoever it was to court. Anyway, it was all quite trivial, and used to subside in due course. Nothing more than that.'

'No longstanding family or other feuds as far as you know?'

'None.'

'Re Mrs Lang,' Pollard went on after a short pause, 'I gather that Mrs Vickers was highly possessive?'

'This is the thing. She positively flaunted their relationship as though she was demonstrating to the world that she and Dru-silla were all in all to each other. It had a pathetic side.'

'It must have been appallingly bad for the girl.'

'It was. Drusilla used to be brought to see me at intervals, sensibly, as I was her aunt's executor, and it always struck me how immature she was, in spite of her undoubted intelligence. She was smothered by all the excessive care and interest and the demanding affection, of course.'

'Then she went up to Oxford, grew up overnight, and the inevitable happened?' queried Pollard.

'Exactly. Tension soon began to develop, but I must say I didn't expect the balloon to go up quite so dramatically. My God, I shall never forget Mrs Vickers arriving at the office the morning she got the letter from Drusilla saying that she was married.'

'I suppose the Langs *are* married? I wondered if Mrs Vickers somehow found out that they were merely living together, and it was this which sparked off the final row. I thought they were unconvincing about the reason for it when I talked to them just now.'

Mr Partridge looked interested.

'It's an idea. When Mrs Vickers was being hysterically vindic-tive on Friday morning, I began to wonder if by any chance Drusilla was actually her child. Illegitimate, of course.'

'We'll be able to clear up both points,' Pollard told him. 'I've set enquiries going on the whole party. I'll let you know the outcome.'

'Thanks. Have another beer. Whether the Langs are married or not,' Mr Partridge resumed when the glasses were refilled, 'Mrs Vickers had something up her sleeve, which seems likely to have been connected with them. At the end of our interview on Friday she instructed me to find her a reliable private enquiry agent.'

'Without telling you what she wanted the chap for?'

'Yes. She made it clear that she'd no intention of letting me in on it. My stock was low at that point. She'd just blown her top, actually.'

Pollard seized the opportunity of broaching a delicate subject.

'Can I take it that she was annoyed with you because of your reaction to the proposed alteration to her will? Mrs Lang told me just now that she'd been disinherited.'

There was a pause.

'Under the circumstances,' Mr Partridge said, 'I'm prepared to give you any information you ask for about my late client's testamentary dispositions. On Friday morning she instructed me to draw up a fresh will for her, leaving her entire estate to charities.'

'Did you do this on the spot?' asked Pollard, with a sense of approaching the heart of the matter.

'I did not. I thought it an outrageous step on her part. I attempted to discuss it, which merely resulted in her threatening to take her business to someone else. I then decided on delaying tactics, and said I would look up suitable charities before drafting the new will, and would let her know when it was ready for her to come in and sign. In the end she accepted this, but wasn't best pleased. She was the kind of client who always wanted everything done at top speed. Like yourself, I felt that there was no convincing explanation of what had caused the explosion, and I hoped that things might calm down.'

'So,' said Pollard thoughtfully, 'Mrs Lang still inherits under the existing will?'

'She does.'

'Is it a substantial estate?'

'I shouldn't be surprised,' replied Mr Partridge cautiously, 'if it comes out eventually at something between fifty and sixty thousand pounds. Net, of course.'

'I asked Mrs Lang how she could know for a fact that Mrs Vickers had disinherited her,' Pollard resumed without comment, 'and she admitted that she was assuming that her aunt did what she had said she was going to do—contact yourself and alter her will immediately she got home. Did she try to make an appointment earlier than last Friday? From what both you and Mrs Lang say the delay seems hardly in character.'

'Yes, she did. She rang the office just before we closed on

Tuesday evening. According to my secretary she was very agitated, and said she must see me urgently. When she heard I was away, I gather she hit the roof. She flatly refused to see either of my partners, though, and insisted on being given the first appointment on Friday morning, the day I was expected back.'

'Will there be a record of that telephone call?' Pollard asked. 'It could be important.'

Mr Partridge gave him a shrewd look.

'I can see that,' he said drily. 'Yes, there'll be a record.'

On leaving Marton Pollard drove on to Highcastle for a hurried snack. He then called in at police headquarters to ask if any message had come through from the Yard. None had, and on learning that a local youth was helping with enquiries into the stabbing case, he took to the road again, feeling envious of Dart's rapid progress.

He soon found himself in a long stream of leisurely Sunday afternoon drivers making for Redbay, resigned himself to crawling, and began to mull over the morning's interviews. Audrey Vickers could hardly have got back to her home on Tuesday much before she rang Partridge's office, say, just on five-thirty pm. So she certainly hadn't wasted much time in setting about making a new will. This lent credibility to Drusilla Lang's alleged belief that she had been disinherited with extreme promptitude, but only up to a certain point. Had she really believed that Partridge would rush through a new will virtually on demand? She knew something of the old boy, and might very well have surmised that he'd play for time. And if she were guilty, she was quite sharp enough to realize the value of eliminating the obvious motive for her aunt's murder.

At this point the road widened sufficiently to allow Pollard to overtake the cars immediately ahead, but he soon arrived at the tail of another bunch, and had to slow down once more.

It was interesting, he thought, that Partridge, too, had been struck by the absence of a convincing explanation of that last catastrophic row between Audrey Vickers and the Langs. It was true that the former wasn't far off being unbalanced at times, and hadn't been feeling well in Athens, but surely there simply must have been more to it than her being hipped at the young couple going off sightseeing on their own.

Pollard literally sat up, and hastily stepped on the brake as the car shot forward several yards. Of all the fools, he thought ... Why on earth hadn't Olivia Strode occurred to him right away?

For a brief moment he was back in his worrying case at Affacombe some years earlier. He was facing Olivia Strode across the tea-table in her cottage at Affacombe, a village about twenty miles from Highcastle. She was answering his questions with intelligence and composure. Then, quite suddenly, her habit of observation stimulated by her interest in local history had resulted in her giving him, quite unconsciously, that tiny vital clue ...

This could be it, he thought, reverting to the present. Drusilla Lang had said that Olivia Strode was around when Mrs Vickers was taken ill on the Acropolis, offered to help, and got slapped down for her pains. This was bound to have aroused her interest in the trio, and anyway the incident would have become a talking point on the ship. He'd ring her, and ask if he might run over to Affacombe. There was a sporting chance that she would be able to throw some light on what had happened between Audrey Vickers and the Langs. Better not mention the idea to Dart, though. Pollard grinned to himself, remembering the suspicion and resentment with which the latter had regarded Olivia's involuntary involvement in the Affacombe affair.

A few minutes later he drew up outside Lauriston, dispersing a group of ghoulish sightseers. Pointedly ignoring them, he strode up the garden path and was admitted to the house by Toye.

'Any luck?' Pollard asked, as the front door closed behind them.

'Nothing useful so far,' Toye told him, indicating neat little heaps of papers on the dining-room table. 'That lot's out of the bureau. Everything in good order and clipped together: she was businesslike all right. Just receipts, things like her telly licence, minutes of some local committees, a lot of stuff about the cruise and one or two personal letters of the trivial sort. I've checked through the address book and the list of telephone numbers she'd made, but none of the names match up with anybody on the passsenger list. There was a good stock of stationery and stamps, and that's the lot. I've been through the rest of the ground-floor rooms, and there's nothing for us there either, unless you count a sort of sidelight on the lady's state of mind. Take a look at these, sir.'

Pollard followed him across the hall to the oak chest, where a pile of dusty framed photographs of Drusilla Lang had been stacked.

'Found 'em at the back of the cupboard under the stairs,' Toye explained.

Pollard studied them with interest. The sequence recorded Drusilla's evolution from small child to schoolgirl, and on to adolescent and undergraduate. Some were studio portraits and others enlarged snapshots. Several showed her with her aunt. Pollard picked out one of these.

'This one would look perfectly right pinned up in a glass showcase outside a theatre,' he remarked. 'Mrs Audrey Vickers playing the devoted aunt in *We Belong Together*. Judging from the dust I should think the whole lot were weeded out and dumped in the cupboard some time ago. Probably at the time of the Lang marriage last summer. Rejection retorts to rejection, I suppose. Have you had a look round upstairs yet? If only the woman had kept a diary or all her old letters.'

'Not yet, sir. I was on my way up when I heard the car.'

It was Pollard who discovered the locked deed-box in the linen-cupboard. After experimenting with various keys from the key-ring in Audrey Vickers' handbag they opened it hopefully, but the contents were disappointing. There were some pieces of good old-fashioned jewellery, a passport, a bank statement showing a very comfortable credit balance and a copy of her will. Pollard had just begun to read this when the telephone rang. Toye answered it, and reported that it was Highcastle with a message from the Yard.

Pollard took the call on the extension in Audrey Vickers' bedroom, making notes. His eyebrows went up suddenly. Finally he thanked his informant and swung round to Toye.

'So what?' he demanded with some excitement. 'In October 1939 Audrey Vickers—Hurst, as she was then— married a chap called Donald Vickers described as being a member of HM's armed forces. According to Partridge she let it be understood that he'd been killed early on in the war, but there's no record of his death, either in this country or on active service, and he was never reported missing.'

'Walked out on her after he was demobbed, and changed his name, and she was too proud to let on?' Toye suggested.

'Look here,' Pollard said, 'it's just possible we're on to something. I haven't finished telling you everything I got from Partridge this morning. When Audrey Vickers went to see him last Friday morning about changing her will, she asked him to find her a reliable private dick.'

Toye whistled in astonishment.

'Could have been something to do with the Langs, but it ties up with a vanished husband all right. You don't think the chap could have turned up on the same cruise, though, do you, sir? Being the sort of woman she was, she'd have blown her top on the ship, surely? I can't picture her keeping it under her hat till she got home, and then starting enquiries. Besides, he'd have recognized her.'

'We can rule out the *Penelope*, I'm sure,' Pollard said. 'But that's not to say he hadn't been on an earlier cruise—if he's above ground, that is. Suppose there was a photograph of a previous batch of passengers stuck up somewhere, and she spotted him in it, or caught sight of him on a shore trip with a bird in tow?'

'But if this Donald Vickers sent the chocolates, he must have spotted her as well, and somehow found out where she lived,' Toye objected with his usual caution.

'This is true. I know it's all wild speculation at the moment, but the fact remains that her husband may be alive, and this is something worth looking into. I'll get on to the Yard right away about tracing Donald Vickers. As you say, if he walked out on his wife he probably changed his name, and is going under an alias, so finding him may be a job. Anyway, if he was in one of the services it's a starting point.'

Toye went on with his methodical search of the bedrooms, and was presently rejoined by Pollard. After some time they agreed that, short of taking the house to pieces, all possible hiding-places for old diaries and revealing letters had been investigated.

'Looks as though she was determined to forget the past,' Pollard remarked as he shut and locked a window. 'Let's call it a day, shall we, and go and eat?'

They came down stairs to the sitting-room again, and stood looking about them. It faced west, and the early evening sun was flooding in, lighting up the sombre portraits and other pictures on the walls. Pollard's eye was caught by an attractive, if hackneyed water-colour of the Arno and the Ponte Vecchio, and he went over to it for a closer look.

'Pure coincidence, surely,' he said, 'but here's a signature that could be a name on the passenger list. I remember reading it out to the Langs this morning. Bayley. J. Bayley. The less common spelling, and the same initial. Fish out the list, will you?'

While Toye was searching in the file he took down the painting for a closer examination, but it yielded no further information beyond the trade label of a Redbay picture framer on the back.

'Yes, you're quite right, sir,' Toye said. 'B-A-Y-L-E-Y. Mr John Bayley.'

'Never ignore a possible lead, however far-fetched it seems. How old Man Crowe bashed that into me. Before we go I'll just ring the Langs, and ask if John Bayley on the cruise was the artist who painted this thing here.'

An unresponsive Keith Lang answered the telephone, and unwillingly went to fetch his wife. Pollard rightly deduced that both were now feeling decidedly worried and uneasy. On being asked about the water-colour, however, Drusilla seemed relieved, and talked freely.

'It's funny you should ask that,' she said. 'It occurred to Aunt Audrey one day on the cruise. She—well, she was given to, trying to find links with people, and pounced on Mr Bayley one day when we were out on a shore expedition. She went on and on about it, and he got a bit irritable. The more he said he wasn't a painter, the more she insisted he was just being modest. You know.'

'Yes, I see. I gather that she'd never met the water-colour artist, then?'

'Not as far as I know. I was with her when she bought the picture. It was a few years ago, at an art shop in Florence. There were several Bayley things on sale, but he wasn't around himself.'

'Well, thank you very much, Mrs Lang. Sorry to have bothered you.'

He put down the receiver and turned to Toye.

'That's that: she doesn't know of any contact between her aunt and this J. Bayley.'

Later that evening, after a good meal at the Southgate, Pollard and Toye repaired to the room lent to them at police headquarters and brought the case file up to date.

'Well,' Pollard remarked, leaning back in his chair and lighting a cigarette, 'we've covered some quite useful ground today.

Starting with the Langs, we've got the Yard report that Drusilla is Audrey Vickers' niece, and not her illegitimate child, as old Partridge suddenly wondered, and she is married to Keith. We've interviewed the pair, and they hardly seem to fill the bill, but we know that they had the means and the opportunity to put paid to Vickers. Motive's another matter. Vickers did try to see her lawyer and disinherit her niece as soon as she got home, and I don't think it could ever be proved that Drusilla Lang knew there'd been a hold-up over this.'

Toye agreed.

'But we've only got her word for it that she wasn't in touch with Mrs Vickers after they all got back, though,' he added.

'This is it. Well, to continue, we've combed Lauriston, and found nothing that throws any useful light on Audrey Vickers' private life. But we do know that there's no official record of her husband's death. But fair enough, if he deserted her, he probably changed his name. Anyway, if he's around as John Smith he's going to be damn difficult to run to earth, and at present there isn't a shred of evidence to connect him with his wife's murder. We've found a water-colour signed J. Bayley at Lauriston, but he certainly doesn't seem to be the John Bayley of the cruise. Finally,' Pollard paused to expel a mouthful of smoke, 'I've had a Great Thought.'

Toye looked startled.

'The upshot of it was that just now I rang a lady: Mrs Olivia Strode of Affacombe. She's coming in to see us at ten o'clock tomorrow morning. You heard me read out her name from the passenger list, and what Mrs Lang said? That day in Athens when Mrs Vickers came over queer, and she tried to lend a hand, was the day of the row between Mrs V and the Langs. With any luck we might get some information about what actually happened. Could anyone else have been involved, for instance?'

'Funny if Mrs Strode hands us the answer the second time,' commented Toye. 'Lucky she's the reliable sort. Real coincidence she's turned up again in a case.'

'Anyway, it gives us the feeling that we're putting the morning to some use. It's a bit of a nuisance having to hang around here for the inquest, when we could be checking upon the Langs at Fulminster, or pushing ahead with these various enquiries in town. Let's pack it in for tonight, shall we? I think I'll just go and pat Inspector Dart on the back if he's still here.

An arrest within twenty-four hours of that stabbing, the lucky blighter.'

Chief-Inspector Dart was still at his desk, surrounded by papers. He accepted Pollard's congratulations with intense gratification, imperfectly masked by a show of offhandedness.

'Tying up the loose ends?' Pollard asked him. 'I should have thought you were due for an evening off and a celebration.'

'This is that ruddy arson business the CC mentioned last night,' Dart replied. 'Ten days ago Brede House was burnt down at Roccombe, a little town thirty miles or so from here. They found a body in the wreckage. The forensic chaps were called in, and they've reported that it was arson beyond a doubt.'

'Has the body been identified?' Pollard asked, trying to show sympathetic interest.

'No trouble there. It was a local drunk and layabout, with no fixed abode. The place was empty, and it looks as though he was sleeping rough in one of the upstairs rooms. Flat out, I don't doubt, and was suffocated by the smoke. The inquest's been adjourned, but it doesn't look like foul play. I don't suppose whoever started the fire had a clue he was there.'

'What do you think was the idea behind the arson? The insurance money?'

'More likely vandals, the local chaps think. The house had been empty for some time—up for sale, and hanging on hand. The owner wanted to sell to a supermarket chain, who'd have liked to clear the site and expand their present premises, but a preservation order had been put on the house. Picturesque, it was, and full of dry rot, I don't doubt. Anyway, the owner was out of the country.'

A voice cut in over the intercom, announcing a 999 call. Dart swore vigorously, and Pollard seized the opportunity to remove himself, and return to the consideration of his own problems.

SIX

At much the same time that Pollard and Toye drove off from Lauriston, Olivia Strode got a little stiffly to her feet and surveyed the flower-bed which she had just weeded. It was amazing what a state the garden could get into in three weeks, even with Fred Earwaker coming in to cut the grass. All the same she decided to call it a day. Sorting oneself out after a holiday was wearing, and she seemed to have been at it non-stop since arriving home at her cottage at Affacombe on Friday. The only break had been today's lunch with her daughter-in-law's parents, to give them all the latest news of the young people and the grandson.

After putting her tools away Olivia stood for a few moments enjoying the warm May evening. The sky was cloudless, its blueness vividly mirrored in the little river Sinnel flowing quietly at the bottom of the garden. To the north the massive moorland shoulder of Sinneldon crowned with its three barrows was bathed in golden light. I've been a long way and seen marvellous places, she thought, but it's good to come back to this. She turned and walked up the path to the back door of the cottage.

Half an hour later, washed and changed out of her gardening clothes, she settled herself comfortably by the french window of her sitting-room, having first assembled various newspapers and a glass of sherry. A pleasant lethargy descended upon her as she sipped and took an occasional glance round, enjoying being back among her own possessions: books, pictures with their associations, photographs, and the companionable desk at which she had spent so many satisfying hours writing her Parish History of Affacombe. The pile of correspondence awaiting attention wasn't so good, but she'd get down to it in the course of the week ...

Presently the feeling that she really ought to catch up with the news made her pick up the *Scrutator*, her Sunday newspaper. The headlines on the front page reiterated discord and violence abroad and economic malaise at home. She skimmed through several depressing columns, and then glanced at the smaller items at the bottom of the page, the apparently random selection of which always entertained her. ... This week someone in London had won the £25,000 Premium Bond prize. One

65

person out of the huge seething ant heap. She speculated idly as to the kind of person whose life must have been transformed by an enactment of Ernie's. Then her eye was suddenly caught by a local place-name.

REDBAY: SCOTLAND YARD TAKES OVER

'Detective-Superintendent Pollard,' she read, 'has arrived in Redbay to conduct the enquiry into the death by cyanide poisoning of Mrs Audrey Vickers last Friday.'

Olivia's first reaction was incredulity. She read the paragraph for a second, and then for a third time before letting the *Scrutator* drop. She sat staring out into the garden, aware of a gulf between the world now, and the same world a few moments earlier, before she had acquired this unwelcome information... An accident? Was Audrey Vickers the sort of woman to keep cyanide on the premises for dealing with wasps' nests? Dismissing the idea as fantastic, she considered suicide... Definitely a possibility for anyone so overwrought—unbalanced, even. There'd been the break with the Langs, too, after that unfortunate day at Athens, and this might have been the last straw. But surely not cyanide? Audrey Vickers would surely have had a supply of sleeping pills?

Reluctantly Olivia faced the remaining possibility, murder, ominously hinted at by the appearance of Scotland Yard. As memory remorselessly assaulted her senses she felt a shiver at the base of her spine. She saw the promenade deck of the *Penelope* with its pools of light and darkness, and beyond the ship's rail the comings and goings on the shadowy quayside. The composite smell of oil, salt and timber was once again in her nostrils. And just out of sight, away to her left, the Langs were talking, Drusilla passionately, Keith drily. '... She can't stop me getting the money my grandfather left when she does die, and the sooner she does, the better,' Drusilla was saying with fury.

It all came back so sharply that she could feel again the slight constriction of her leg and foot muscles as she tiptoed away out of earshot...

Surfacing with an effort, Olivia tried to think coherently. There was not the smallest reason, she told herself, to get involved. If Drusilla had poisoned her aunt, Pollard would find out. Anyway, why should the murder—if it really was one—link up with the cruise? Audrey Vickers would have been at home for several days. He wouldn't concern himself with her fellow passengers.

She sat on for a few minutes thinking about the Langs, and remembered with discomfort that Drusilla lectured in chemistry somewhere. At this point she got up abruptly, feeling that her evening had been wrecked by the sheer bad luck of having noticed the wretched little paragraph in the *Scrutator*. She'd better have some supper, and try to get the whole thing out of her mind by starting on her letters.

In the kitchen she laid herself a tray, and collected ingredients for an omelette. As she cracked a couple of eggs against the rim of a basin, the saying that you couldn't make an omelette without breaking eggs came into her mind, and simultaneously the telephone rang.

The sudden irrational certainty that Pollard was at the other end made her hand fumble a little as she picked up the receiver.

'Leeford 227,' she said.

'Mrs Olivia Strode?' His voice was surprisingly familiar although she had not heard it for several years.

'Speaking,' she said non-committally, to gain time.

'Good evening Mrs Strode. This is Superintendent Pollard, ringing you from Highcastle.'

'Oh, er, good evening,' she heard herself saying rather weakly.

'You don't sound surprised at my calling you out of the blue, Mrs Strode.'

The implied question was unmistakable. Anyway, what was the point of playing the innocent?

'Not really, Mr Pollard,' she replied. 'I've just seen that paragraph in the *Scrutator*.'

'Good. That saves lengthy explanations. I'll try to be brief. I noticed your name on the passenger list of the cruise Mrs Vickers was on recently, and this morning Mrs Lang told me you had been around when her aunt was taken ill on the Acropolis. For various reasons we're interested in the events of that day, and knowing what an excellent witness you are, I wondered if you'd see me if I ran over to Affacombe tomorrow morning?'

It flashed through Olivia's mind that he might not ask her about anything else.

'Well, if you think I can be of any help,' she said doubtfully.

'I do sympathize. It's extraordinarily bad luck to be caught up in a second police enquiry. Would ten o'clock be too early for you?'

'No.' She hesitated for a moment. 'Actually I was coming in to Highcastle for shopping tomorrow morning. Perhaps it might be better?'

'Quite. I take your point. I don't want to revive unhappy memories in your lovely village. Do you know where police headquarters are?'

'Yes. Shall I come along at ten?'

'That will be fine, Mrs Strode. I'll be on the lookout for you. Goodbye, and thank you.'

'Goodbye,' Olivia said, and heard the click as he rang off.

She returned to the kitchen, to be greeted by the broken eggs, and stared at them. He's braced me up somehow, she thought. After all, ghastly woman though she was, Audrey Vickers had a right to life ... I do hope it wasn't those two, though.

At exactly one minute to ten on the following morning Olivia Strode walked into the Highcastle police headquarters, and Pollard stepped forward to greet her.

'I'm afraid this isn't up to the standard of your cottage,' he said a few moments later, showing her into a small room with bare walls, austerely furnished with a wooden table and three upright chairs. 'I've thought about it more than once. Just the sort of place my wife and I hope to retire to one day.'

She smiled at him as she sat down.

'I'm so glad you like Poldens,' she told him. 'I'm quite dotty about it myself. On the cruise some people at our table got a radiogram to say a house they owned had been burnt down. I immediately got into a panic in case Poldens was struck by lightning or suddenly developed defective wiring.'

He looks a bit older, she thought, and a bit more assured and authoritative. Very much the same, though. It surprised her that he made no attempt to respond to this small talk, but looked at her intently.

'Inspector Dart is enquiring into a recent fire which destroyed a house whose owner was abroad,' he said. 'Do you know where the one you mention took place?'

'I'm afraid I don't,' she told him.

'What was the owner's name?'

'She was a Mrs John Bayley.'

'Was her husband on the cruise with her?'

68

'Yes, he was. They sat at my table, actually.'

'Were either of them painters?'

'I don't think so,' Olivia replied, mystified. 'Several people on board painted quite a lot, but I'm pretty sure the Bayleys never did.'

'Just a case of a possible coincidence,' Pollard said, smiling at her. 'I expect you remember Inspector Dart?'

'Indeed I do,' Olivia replied with amusement. 'He regarded me with a deep suspicion all through the Affacombe trouble. But why a police enquiry into this fire?'

'It's usual, when a house is unoccupied, and there's no apparent explanation of a fire. And in this case there was a further reason. A man's body was found in the ruins.'

Olivia gave a horrified exclamation.

'How dreadful! What can have happened?'

'The forensic experts have found out that the fire was started deliberately. The man—a local drop-out—seems to have been upstairs, probably sleeping it off, and suffocated by smoke. It looks as though whoever set the place alight didn't know he was there.'

'Vandals, I expect. Empty houses seem to draw them like magnets. Where was it? I only got home on Friday, and haven't caught up with local news yet.'

'At Roccombe. Brede House, it was called.'

'Oh, no!' she exclaimed. 'Not the lovely little seventeenth-century timber-framed house, with the external staircase turret? It's recently been listed ... I expect you think I'm heartless to mind so much about the house.'

'I don't. I'm interested in old houses myself. But may we hark back to the fire you told me about? I'd just like to check up on the owner's name with Inspector Dart. If it turns out that he's investigating your Mrs Bayley's fire, obviously he'd be glad of a word with you. Could you face it? It would only take a few minutes, and then we can get down to our own business.'

'You're impossibly persuasive, Mr Pollard. If it wasn't a serious matter the situation would be comic, you know.'

'I'll go and see if he wants to come along,' Pollard said, getting to his feet. He paused at the door with a grin. 'He's now Chief-Inspector, by the way. Promotion often mellows.'

Left alone, Olivia realized that the unexpected diversion had taken any remaining tension out of her interview with Pollard. It would be extraordinary if two of the cruise passengers had been involved in disasters in the neighbourhood. There seemed very little that she could tell Inspector Dart if Brede House had been Mrs Bayley's, all the same.

Apparently it had. She could hear the returning footsteps and conversation, and found herself greeting a self-conscious Dart with tactful congratulations on his Chief-Inspectorship.

After a lengthy preamble he asked her if she could confirm that Mr and Mrs Bayley had been on the cruise throughout.

'You'll understand that under the circumstances this is the sort of question we have to ask,' he said. 'We'll be getting on to the Company, of course, but since you're here, Mrs Strode, and they were at your table, it's a chance of first-hand information.'

Olivia was able to assure him categorically that the Bayleys had been with the cruise party during the whole period up to the ship's return to Venice.

'Looking back on it, I'm sure they didn't miss a single meal or shore excursion,' she said.

'That's that, then,' Dart remarked with satisfaction. 'Now, I understand you were with Mr and Mrs Bayley when the radiogram from their solicitor about the fire reached them?'

'Yes, I was. We were at dinner, on the day when we were berthed at Piraeus, in Greece.'

As she spoke, she noticed that Pollard, hitherto a discreetly amused spectator, registered distinct interest.

'Perhaps you'd describe the incident in your own words, Mrs Strode?'

Olivia shut her eyes for a moment, opened them again, and proceeded to give a succinct account of the radiogram's arrival and the Bayleys' reactions.

Dart made some notes, read them over and frowned.

'Would you say the news was a shock to Mr and Mrs Bayley?' he asked.

'Nothing as strong as that. After all it wasn't their home. They were a bit startled, but mostly annoyed, I think, at the prospect of bother with the insurance people, and perhaps having to cut short their stay in Venice, and fly straight home.'

'And did they? Fly straight home?'

'Someone else at our table said they had. Apparently they rang their solicitor when we got to Venice, and he advised them to come back at once. I suppose it was known about the body by then. I didn't see them go off. We had a final day in Venice, and I went ashore early and didn't get back until dinner time.'

In reply to further questions from Dart, Olivia described the Bayleys to the best of her ability. No, she didn't know what Mr Bayley's job was, but his wife had referred to the factory on one occasion, so he was probably in industry.

Inspector Dart gathered his papers together, and brought the interview to a close, thanking her warmly for her help.

'All is now forgiven,' Pollard remarked as the door closed. 'Some elevenses, I think, don't you? Canteen coffee, or would you feel safer with tea?'

As they waited for a tray of tea to be brought, he talked easily, making enquiries after mutual acquaintances in Affacombe. When it arrived he asked her if she would pour out.

'You don't smoke, do you? Will it worry you if I do?'

'Not a scrap,' she replied, handing him his cup.

'This question is getting monotonous,' he said, 'but it's essential to keep on asking it. What sort of a person was Audrey Vickers? You're a writer and a broadcaster. I want you to put her over as convincingly as you can.'

Olivia slowly drank some tea. Into her mind came a vivid picture of Audrey Vickers, restless-eyed and talking volubly.

'You've—you've seen her, I expect?' she asked.

'I've seen the body, yes. It helps one to reconstruct, you know. I once had a case which started off with a bare skeleton, and felt very stuck.'

'She was a woman completely out of touch with reality as far as her relationships with other people went. More than anyone I've ever met. She gave me the impression of having run away from it for so long that she'd lost the power of recognizing it. She'd built up a kind of fantasy world in this connection, and the strain of trying to maintain it made her absolutely self-absorbed and perpetually on the defensive. Neurotic, too, as a sort of side-effect.'

Pollard, listening intently, gave a nod of comprehension.

'She was quite a forceful person by temperament,' Olivia went on thoughtfully, 'so she expressed her defensiveness aggressively, if I can put it like that. Pushing herself forward all the time, and being insanely possessive of her niece, who is her only near relative, I believe. And, of course, a result of this was her hostility to Mr Lang. You can understand what an unpopular member of the cruise she was, particularly because of her treatment of the young people. She'd never let them off the lead for a moment if she could help it. You'd hear other passengers

71

saying how they'd managed to avoid her—I did myself, on occasions. But I admit I felt bad about it sometimes. She was obviously an acutely unhappy woman. Is this the sort of thing you want, by the way?'

'Exactly what I want,' Pollard assured her. 'But you didn't always avoid her, did you? Mrs Lang told me how you tried to come to the rescue when her aunt felt ill on the Acropolis.'

'I'm afraid I wasn't moved by concern for Mrs Vickers. I was furious at her insisting on the Langs taking her back to the ship before they'd even had time to look around.'

'Didn't you think Mrs Vickers really was ill?'

'No, I didn't. My reaction was that the stuffy heat and pretty steep climb up from the coach park had made her a bit breathless, and that she was putting on an act. You see, she had been perfectly all right a few minutes earlier. The three of them were right on my heels as we came up, and she was talking in her usual vociferous way. Incidentally, the ship's doctor couldn't find anything wrong with her when he saw her.'

'Did she usually enjoy the visits to the sites?' Pollard asked.

'Not really for their own sake, I think. I feel I'm being completely feline, but it seemed to me she used them as opportunities for getting into conversation with people, and generally pushing herself.'

'Then isn't it odd that she shammed illness and contracted out on the Acropolis? It must have been the most popular site of the whole trip.'

'Yes, it is,' Olivia agreed. 'It hadn't struck me in that light.'

'You say they were just behind you. Did this illness, genuine or otherwise, come on very suddenly?'

'I don't know that I can answer that question. You see, my one aim was not to get involved with them: I'd pretended not to notice they were behind me. The way out on to the top was blocked by a party of noisy Americans. There was an American cruise ship in, too, and the crowds were really rather trying. I pushed past, and slipped away to the right. Then, at last, I was able to register the Parthenon. . . . I suppose it was a minute or two before I surfaced again, and started off to look at the Erectheum, over on the left. It was just at that moment that I heard Mrs Vickers demanding to be taken back to the ship at once, and saw her sitting down with her hand to her heart, looking a bit flushed.'

Pollard considered, trying to visualize the scene.

'Could she have had a breeze with the Americans?'

Olivia screwed up her eyes and thought hard.

'I don't think so. I dimly remember hearing their conversation going on and on while I was looking at the Parthenon.'

'I suppose you don't remember what they were talking about?'

'I do, as it happens. If I hadn't been feeling exasperated by the noise and masses of people, I should have been amused. There were three women who hadn't met for some time—college contemporaries, I gathered. They had all married in the meantime, and were showing off their husbands to each other with cries of excitement. It was all rather disjointed, but I do remember one saying that she'd urged hers to take American citizenship.'

As Pollard made no comment Olivia looked up, to find him deep in thought, an inscrutable expression on his face. She waited patiently. His next question mystified her.

'You say that an American cruise ship was in at the same time as yours. Can you remember her name?'

Feeling that this was really rather unreasonable, she shook her head.

'I don't think I ever took it in.'

'What time did the Langs return to the *Penelope* that night?' he asked, changing the subject.

'I can't tell you that, either. They weren't at dinner, at any rate.'

'So you didn't see them again on that day?'

'No.' This was the literal truth, but she had hesitated fractionally, and knew that Pollard was aware of it.

'According to Mrs Lang, the row which led to the final breach between her and her aunt took place after she and her husband got back. Did you know this at the time, Mrs Strode?'

'Well, yes, I did, actually,' she replied, avoiding his eye. 'About half-past eleven I was strolling round the deck by myself and accidentally overheard a conversation between the Langs. They didn't know I was just out of sight. The gist of it was that Mrs Vickers had said things to Mr Lang that his wife felt she couldn't forgive, and she had decided to have nothing more to do with her aunt. Mr Lang was trying to lower the temperature.'

'I'm very glad you've told me about this,' Pollard said. 'It's valuable confirmation of what seemed an unconvincing story. Was anything said about the possibility of Mrs Vickers altering her will?'

'Yes. Mrs Lang said Mrs Vickers could leave her money to a cats' home if she liked. Then there was something about money from a grandfather having to come to her.'

'Did Mrs Lang utter any threats towards Mrs Vickers?' Pollard shot the question abruptly.

Olivia raised her head and looked at him straight in the face. 'No. She definitely did not utter threats. She remarked that she wished Mrs Vickers really had a weak heart instead of pretending she had, and that the sooner she died, the better. But this was shooting her mouth, as my son would put it. There was nothing well, purposeful, in the way she said it.'

There was another pause.

'You've been most patient with me, Mrs Strode,' Pollard told her. 'One more question and then I really am through. Did you notice any special contact between Mrs Vickers and anybody else on the *Penelope*?'

'None. As I told you, people's reaction was to avoid her as far as they possibly could.'

A decision taken by Pollard in the watches of the night had sent Toye on ahead to Fulminster, to check the Langs' statements about their movements on returning from the cruise. He travelled by train, and on arrival went to the police station. A previous case of Pollard's had involved contacts with Fulminster, and Toye was welcomed with interest, and offers of any assistance he wanted. He learnt that neither of the Langs was known to the police, and that their address suggested that they were living in part of one of the older houses on the former outskirts of the city, now largely converted into flats. Toye gratefully accepted an offer to run him up to the place, and was set down in a quiet road about a mile from the city centre. It was flanked by tall houses of red brick with semi-basements and regrettable excrescences such as cupolas. There were small gardens in front, most of which now appeared to be used as car ports. Toye noted that Number Eleven, the address given by the Langs, was in reasonably good shape. There were three bells outside the front door, each surmounted by a card in a slot. After inspecting these, Toye came to the conclusion that the semi-basement and second floor had been let to H. Meadfoot and K. Lang respectively, and rang the middle bell under A. C. Porter.

The door was opened by a greyhaired man wearing a boiler-suit splashed with paint. He looked enquiringly at Toye.

'If it's my wife you want, she's out shopping,' he said.

Toye once again presented his credentials.

'Mr Porter, sir?' he enquired politely. 'The owner of the house? I'd be glad of a word with you.'

Surprise on Mr Porter's face was followed by comprehension.

'Come in, Sergeant,' he said. 'Sorry we're in a bit of a mess. I'm doing a spot of house decorating. Mind coming into the kitchen? It's about the Langs, I expect? Shocking business.'

They sat down at a table in the window, and Toye explained that he was making a purely routine check in connection with the death of Mrs Audrey Vickers of Redbay, aunt of Mrs Lang.

'I understand that your tenants got back from their holiday last Tuesday?' he asked.

'That's quite correct,' replied Mr Porter. 'They turned up about half-past eight. My wife had got something keeping hot in the oven for their supper. Not part of the bond, of course, but they're a nice young couple, and we like to do them a kindness in and out.'

'Were they at home all the next day, sir?'

'Let me see. That would be Wednesday. Mrs Lang went off to the college after breakfast as usual. At least, that's where I imagine she went. They'd said something about having run it rather fine for the beginning of her term. I saw Lang coming in with a shopping basket before lunch. He's around most of the time. Writes, you know. He hasn't made much of a success of it so far, but a publisher's just taken a novel he's written. They were both in later in the evening, and seemed to be tramping round overhead half the night. We're early bedders, and I suppose we noticed them more after three weeks' peace. They're quiet enough, but of course the house wasn't built to be turned into flats. We wanted to go on living in it when I retired, though, so letting off part of it was the obvious solution.'

Asked about Thursday, Mr Porter remembered that both the Langs had been out all day. He clearly recalled Mr Lang going off for an interview with his prospective publisher in London.

'He's a sober sort of chap as a rule, but he seemed quite excited. I wished him luck, and he said he'd got another type-script in his case which he was going to get them to have a look at.'

Friday had apparently been a perfectly normal day, with Mr

Lang's typewriter going full blast. Then, on Saturday, the police had come with the news about Mrs Vickers. Mrs Porter had been quite upset.

Having got all the information he wanted, Toye gratified Mr Porter's curiosity with a few unimportant details about the murder. Then, thanking him for his help, he managed to extract himself.

Just as he was leaving a thought struck him.

'Have Mr and Mrs Lang a telephone?' he asked.

'No. We agreed when they came that they could use ours in any emergency, but except for when they were both ill last winter, it's never arisen as far as I know.'

Toye thanked Mr Porter once again, and departed in the direction of the gate.

It was already after twelve, and he decided to leave the Technical College until after lunch. He walked back to the centre of Fulminster, prospected carefully, and was soon enjoying a most satisfactory meal of grilled lamb chops, preceded by tomato soup, and followed by apple pie and custard. He calculated that with the inquest at Redbay not starting until half-past two, Pollard could hardly drive up to collect him before half-past four. There would be plenty of time to check up on Mrs Lang at the Tech, write up his notes, and take a look round.

He arrived at the Technical College shortly before two. The entrance hall reminded him of a London railway terminus in the rush hour. For a few fascinated minutes he watched the concentration of bizarre hair-styles, beard and other hirsute adornments, maxis, minis, midis and male attire which baffled classification. No one took the slightest notice of him, although he narrowly escaped being knocked down on several occasions. Then electric bells rang stridently, and the crowd thinned out as if by magic. He advanced on a counter labelled 'Enquiries', and asked to speak to someone in authority.

There was a flutter among the young women on duty, and a more senior figure emerged from an inner room.

Once again Toye went through the routine of establishing his identity, and explained that he merely wanted confirmation of Mrs Lang's presence in the College during the latter part of the previous week. After a good deal of internal telephoning he was informed that Dr Leadbitter, Head of the Department of Chemistry, would see him when he had finished lecturing. He was escorted by way of a lift and endless corridors to the science block, and asked to wait in Dr Leadbitter's room. He contemplated its incredible untidiness with interest, wondering how anyone who lived in the midst of such chaos could cope with the intricate accuracies of advanced scientific techniques. At last the door opened, and a small fair man came in.

Dr Leadbitter was dry and sparing of speech. He listened without comment to Toye's request for information, and stated that Mrs Lang had carried out her normal duties on the Wednesday, Thursday and Friday of the previous week.

'That is to say, she was present in this building from approximately eight forty-five am to one pm and two pm to five pm. I do not know where she lunched. To save time, I will add that she has access to cyanide. So have I, and the other members of my staff. It does not follow that any of us are murders. I do not think I can usefully tell you anything else, Sergeant.'

His thanks cut short, Toye found himself outside in the corridor, with a feeling of having been catapulted into space. With some difficulty he found his way to the ground floor, noticing en route a number of isolated telephone boxes. Leading off the entrance hall was a row of half a dozen of them.

Deciding that the city Library would be a convenient place for writing up his notes, he made his way there, and settled down in a quiet corner of the reference section. The gist of what he had to report was complete confirmation of the Langs' statements. There were two small points of interest, though. The pair had been up very late on Wednesday night, disturbing the Porters. If cyanide had been brought back from the College, this would have been the time when the chocolates were doctored. And when Lang went to London on Thursday morning, he took a case which could have contained the parcel for posting. Neither of these things was evidence. Just pointers, Toye thought.

He sat on, meditating. Means and opportunity, he thought, but so far the money motive, the only convincing one, wasn't anything like established. The fact that Mrs Vickers had tried to contact her solicitor as soon as she got home was a point in Mrs Lang's favour. It certainly looked as though she had good reason to believe that her aunt was taking immediate steps to cut her out. But did a bright young woman like Mrs Lang think that solicitors drew up wills involving quite a bit of money just on demand, so to speak? Of course it could be done, but she'd met Mr Partridge, and must have known that he was the cautious type, not a bit likely to let himself be stampeded into action.

As he meditated, the telephone boxes at the Technical College returned to Toye's mind. Suppose Mrs Lang had rung the solicitor's office sometime on Wednesday, to ask him if he could do anything about her being cut out of the will? They'd have told her he was away, and not available until Friday, and this meant a couple of days' delay. Of course there was the possibility of her aunt having seen one of the partners, but perhaps this would have been so out of character that Mrs Lang felt it could safely be discounted? Or her husband could have rung from a call box somewhere. STD call probably, making it harder, but not impossible to trace.

Toye made a few more notes before leaving the library. In his careful thorough way he inspected a telephone directory in a kiosk, and found that an STD call could be put through to Highcastle from Fulminster. This done, he decided that there was plenty of time for a look round before Pollard could possibly arrive to pick him up, and set off in the direction of the Cathedral. Strains of organ music were seeping through the north door. He went quietly inside, and slipped into a chair by a pillar.

The remote singing and chanting in the choir and the vast tranquil spaces of the nave were soothing. . . . He came to with a start as the tail of the robed procession was disappearing, and scrambled hastily to his feet, alarmed to find that it was a quarter past four. Leaving the Cathedral he set off briskly for the police station. Not far short of it there was a toot in his ear, and Pollard drew up with a grin. Toye got in beside him hastily.

'You must've stepped on it, sir,' he said.

'The inquest proceedings were an all-time speed record. I did scorch a bit, though. Where do we park?'

'Turn in and bear right, round the buildings.'

A few minutes later they drew up. Pollard switched off the engine, and stretched himself.

'Well,' he said, 'it looks as though we may have had a break. If Audrey Vickers didn't collide head on with her husband and his bigamous bride on the Acropolis, I'll go back to pounding a beat.'

Toye stared at him incredulously.

'I'm dead serious,' Pollard assured him. 'Listen to what I got from Mrs Strode this morning. . . .'

He produced almost verbatim Olivia Strode's description of the party of Americans blocking her exit from the Processional Way on to the Acropolis.

'If,' he concluded, 'the chap who was advised to take American citizenship by his unsuspecting bride is Donald Vickers, and Audrey Vickers took the situation in, no wonder she was blown off course, took it out on the Langs that night, and started looking for an enquiry agent as soon as she got home. It makes sense, Toye, you've got to admit.'

SEVEN

At ten o'clock that same evening Pollard finished a late supper with a contented sigh, pushed away his empty plate, and looked across the kitchen at his wife who was busy with preparations for the next morning.

'Can't think how you manage it,' he said. 'Hot meals like this at all hours.'

'Elementary, my dear Watson,' Jane replied. 'An oil-fired Aga, and a kitchen big enough for civilized eating as well as cooking.'

'You're tired, though. Natural smudges under the eyes.'

'It's only lack of sleep. Andrew's first molar's coming through. I was up with him quite a bit last night.'

'If he starts yelling tonight, I'm taking over, then. I was jolly good when they were both cutting their first teeth at the same time. Remember?'

'We'll see about that,' Jane replied non-committally, beginning to clear the table. 'You've got your own job to cope with. Just bung all this into the dishwasher, will you, while I go and take up the twins? Then we can relax in peace in the sitting-room. I'm dying to hear about The Case of the Poisoned Chocolates.'

'Wouldn't some sleep be better for you?'

'Definitely not. My tiredness is mainly psychosomatic, due to lack of social intercourse. Assunta's shaping well, but her English is still about as basic as my Italian. Still, we're luckier than most to get two good au pairs in a row.'

Stretched out in his favourite armchair Pollard watched her

come in ten minutes later, curl up on the settee, and arrange a dark green cushion behind her head.

'That colour's the perfect background for red–gold hair,' he remarked.

'Naturally I work out that sort of thing. Wasn't I a lecturer in a college of art until maternity clamped down on me? Pray proceed, Detective-Superintendent Pollard.'

She wriggled into a still more comfortable position, and looked at him enquiringly.

'In October 1939,' Pollard began, 'at a London registry office, Audrey Joan Hurst, spinster, aged twenty-four, married Donald James Vickers, bachelor, aged twenty-eight, serving in HM armed forces. They spent a short honeymoon at Redbay—at least, that's what she told the vicar. I had a natter with him before the inquest this afternoon. After the war she reappeared in Redbay as a widow, and settled down there. But there's no record of her husband's death, either on active service or in this country. Neither was he a POW or reported missing. He was demobbed, and the rest seems to have been silence.'

'This,' Jane said happily, 'is super. . . .'

Pollard's closely reasoned narrative took some time.

'You know, you do have luck,' Jane said, when it came to an end. 'This Mrs Strode turning up again, for instance. It simply isn't true.'

'Of course, we don't know yet that it is true—that Donald Vickers was in that party of Americans on the Acropolis.'

'I realize that. But it does seem to fit, doesn't it? I mean, it makes some sense of the way Audrey Vickers behaved afterwards. A jolt like that would be more than enough to send anyone of her type over the edge, and the Langs walking out on her would have been the end. She'd have to take it out on somebody, and they were the obvious people.'

'Always assuming that one of the chaps was Vickers, I agree that it all goes a long way to explain the bust-up, which otherwise seems to have come out of the blue. Her asking Partridge to lay on an enquiry agent could fit in, too.'

'How are you finding out if Donald Vickers did take American nationality after the war?' Jane asked.

'The Yard's contacted the British Embassy in Washington, and they'll get on to whatever department of the Federal Government it is. Ministry of the Interior, I should think. With luck we might hear something tomorrow.'

Jane rolled over on to her back, clasped her hands behind her head, and stared at the ceiling.

'Mightn't Donald Vickers have got hold of a faked passport after he was demobbed, and taken out naturalization papers under an assumed name?'

'There,' Pollard replied, 'you've put your finger through one of the gaping holes in the potential case against him, as it stands at present. But if he was a carefree sort of bloke he mightn't have thought it necessary to cover his tracks to that extent. There was a good old churn-up going on just then. And the States must have seemed much more remote before regular supersonic air services.'

'Audrey Vickers must have had money,' Jane said reflectively 'I suppose Donald felt he couldn't face life with her, all the same.'

'She may have come in for it later, of course. What's all this clicking of the gate?'

'Assunta and her boyfriend saying goodnight. Eleven's her deadline. Not to worry. They're both most devout, and she's taken him to see the Sisters at the convent on the Downs. There's a Mother Francis there who speaks Italian. Here she comes. I'll just let her in, and see if she wants a snack before she goes to bed.'

While waiting for Jane to come back, Pollard lit a cigarette, and subsided into his chair once more, a slight frown on his face.

'We've got the name of the American cruise ship from the port authorities at Piraeus,' he resumed, when she was settled to listen again. 'But I don't think the Vickers pair—again, assuming we're really concerned with them—could have been passengers. It sailed for Istanbul on the Friday afternoon. If Vickers sent those chocolates, he'd got to get hold of them in the first place. Honeydew is a very small concern, and although we'll be checking up on it tomorrow, I'm sure their stuff wouldn't be on sale in Greece. Much more likely that the Vickers were on some other tour, or even travelling independently, and flew back to London. We're trying Athens airport, and the hotels.'

'When you think of the resources of the Yard, it's amazing that anybody manages to slip through the net,' Jane observed.

'Unfortunately the world's quite a place, relative to the size of a wanted chap,' Pollard replied rather gloomily.

Silence descended. Turning her head slightly, Jane contemplated her husband with interest.

'Even allowing that we're on to Vickers, there are terrific hurdles ahead,' he said at last. 'For one thing, how does an American tourist get hold of cyanide at short notice? It isn't the sort of simple remedy you carry around with you.'

'Are you hot on his trail because you think he did send the chocolates,' Jane said slowly, 'or because you're convinced the Langs didn't, and no other likely candidate has turned up?'

Pollard suddenly grinned.

'What a one you are for hitting the nail on the head! See what comes of marrying an intelligent woman with a trained mind. If Donald recognized Audrey, and realized that she'd recognized him, he'd have the whale of a motive for liquidating her, of course. And a reasonable opportunity, provided that he could get himself back to London in the ordinary course of events. The stumbling-block where he's concerned is the means of cooking the chocolates. On the other hand, the Langs had means and opportunity beyond doubt, and it's quite possible that Drusilla found out that the will hadn't been altered as soon as she expected and so the money motive still stood. But I just can't see those two sticking out their necks in that utterly obvious way. They're too intelligent. And unless I've completely lost my eye, too fundamentally decent to have engineered a death like that. Cyanide poisoning is pretty foul.'

'People who are highly intelligent academically can be complete fools in other spheres.'

'That's true, and it's what's really biting me. Hell! I hate this case. I can't see my way ahead, and I know perfectly well that pressure's building up to make me pull in the Langs. I've got to report to the AC tomorrow.'

'What you need is a good night's sleep,' Jane remarked. 'I can do with one, too. Let's go up.'

In the first faint morning greyness Pollard was roused by a pathetic wail. Jane was already half out of bed, but he pulled her back.

'Lie down, and go to sleep again,' he said firmly.

She subsided with some inarticulate words, and he grabbed a dressing-gown and made for the twins' room. Scooping up Andrew, he was relieved to find him dry: somehow the intrica-

82

cies of nappy-changing were more difficult to carry through by artificial light. He wrapped the cot blanket round the small form, and hurried out before Rose woke up too. The wail stopped, and Andrew showed signs of interest in his unexpected rescuer.

'Your toothache,' Pollard informed him as they went downstairs, 'is mainly psychosomatic, due to lack of social intercourse. . . .'

He settled his son comfortably in the crook of his left arm, cradled against him, and paced slowly up and down the sittingroom, patting him gently on the back. Andrew began to respond with small contented sounds.

Amid the blurred shapes of the pre-dawn world Pollard suddenly felt his thinking about his case clarify. The whole Acropolis business could so well turn out to be a mare's nest, in spite of Olivia Strode's possibly relevant recollections. And Audrey Vickers had been quite unbalanced enough to give way to a sadistic impulse to spoil the Langs' enjoyment. Then, when they hit back, all her built-up resentment against Drusilla could very well have boiled over. Wasn't all this a much more convincing explanation of the row than dragging in a fantastic coincidence? And re the Langs, he reminded himself, what a policeman thinks isn't evidence, unless supported by hard facts. . . . Unless it was established quickly and beyond doubt that the two Vickers had met that day, the lead had better be shelved and the case against the Langs pursued. A visit to the Honeydew shop with that recent photograph of Drusilla brought from Lauriston was obviously a priority. . . .

Realizing that Andrew was completely inert and deep in sleep, Pollard carried him carefully upstairs and returned him to his cot without rousing him.

On his arrival at the Yard six hours later, Pollard learnt that no information had come in from Washington overnight. After dealing with some urgent matters connected with other cases, he asked his secretary to send in Toye, and began to draw up a provisional programme for the morning.

'We can't afford the time to hang around waiting for Washington,' he said, when Toye put in an appearance. 'We're seeing the Odyssey Tours people at twelve. You've read Longman's report, I take it? Of course they never sent ex-passengers chocolates or anything else, as we knew all along, but it's another point officially cleared up. I want to ask them about their compliments slips. We'll go along to Honeydew in the meantime. Just match up that recent photograph of Mrs Lang with a few others like it, will you? And we'll want the chocolates and the packaging, too.'

'Are we going to the Honeydew factory as well, sir?'

'You can tackle that while I'm with the Odyssey lot. It could be that the postal orders go direct from it.'

Pollard did not miss a look of satisfaction on Toye's face, and the implicaton that he, for one, considered the Langs a much better bet than the still hypothetical Donald Vickers.

Honeydew Ltd occupied the ground floor of a house in Market Court, a cul-de-sac off West Audley Street. Toye manoeuvred the car into a vacant parking-space, and they proceeded on foot. The little street had been rebuilt about a hundred years earlier, and its tall single-fronted houses were now given over to offices and recherché business establishments. Pollard and Toye paused on the pavement outside Honeydew, at Number Seven, to study the window display. The limited space available was draped in golden velvet. A large bowl of crimson peonies set off an austerely plain box bearing the inscription HONEYDEW'S ASSORTMENT SUPREME. In the background a straw skep was perched on a wooden stool.

Toye asked how much that little lot would set you back.

'You wouldn't even ask in a joint like this,' Pollard told him. 'Just shove a fiver across the counter. Let's go in.'

HONEYDEW: PLEASE ENTER, they read on the door to the right of the narrow entrance hall. Painted below the words was a straw skep, similar to the one in the window. Pollard opened the door, and they walked into a room with no resemblance to the popular image of a sweet-shop. It was carpeted to the walls in golden brown, and furnished with elegant tables which functioned as display stands for Honeydew products. There was an unobtrusive counter in a corner. At the back of the room an open door appeared to lead into a store-room, from which a woman came hurrying.

'I'm so sorry, sir,' she said anxiously. 'I didn't hear you come in.'

'We've only just this moment arrived,' he assured her. 'This room is arranged in a very attractive way,' he added, glancing around him.

She was a small woman, little over five feet in height, with a sallow complexion, dark eyes, and hair streaked with grey which she wore in an old-fashioned style with a fringe. As Pollard studied her he saw her beginning to look at him doubtfully. Shrewd, if diffident, he thought. She realizes we aren't the sort to buy chocolates in a place like this.

'I had better explain at once that we aren't customers,' he said. 'We're police officers from New Scotland Yard, engaged on an enquiry in which you may be able to help us. Here's my card. I'm Detective-Superintendent Pollard, and this is Sergeant Toye, my assistant.'

He watched her nervously moisten her lips, as she took the card he held out, but made no attempt to read it.

'There's absolutely nothing for you to be alarmed about, Mrs—er?'

'Willis,' she said faintly.

'Mrs Willis, I assure you. Perhaps we could sit down somewhere?'

With obvious reluctance she moved in the direction of the counter, and indicated the two gilt chairs drawn up to it. Pollard and Toye lowered themselves gingerly on to these, and she sat on the edge of a stool facing them.

'I expect you've read in the papers about the death of a Mrs Audrey Vickers who ate some chocolates containing a poison called cyanide, haven't you?' Pollard asked her.

The relief in her face was unmistakable.

'Yes,' she said almost eagerly. 'What a shocking thing ... why, you'd never think ...'

She broke off, and stared at him.

'You can't mean ... surely ...?'

'I see that you've got there, Mrs Willis. It's exactly what I do mean. The poisoned chocolates arrived in a Honeydew box, and Scotland Yard wants to find out if they were made by this firm. No one is suggesting that they were sent from here, of course.'

'Nothing's sent from here. All the post orders go off from the factory.'

'Quite,' said Pollard soothingly. 'That's what we expected to hear. But we've brought some of the chocolates, and the box they arrived in, and want you to look at them, and see if they are a Honeydew make.'

As he talked, he realized that Mrs Willis was darting anxious glances at the door from the hall.

'Oh, I couldn't take the responsibility,' she said in agitation.

'It isn't my place. I'm only employed here ... I really couldn't, not really. You must see the lady who owns the business. She's Mrs Morse. She——'

She broke off hastily as the door opened.

'Who's asking for me?' demanded a loud feminine voice. 'Here I am. Zoë Morse.'

A tall, big-built woman came in, shutting the door noisily behind her. About fifty, Pollard thought, registering heavy make-up, an assertive bust, and expensive, rather outré clothes.

Pollard got to his feet.

'Good morning,' he said, and introduced Toye and himself. 'You are the owner of Honeydew, Mrs Morse?'

'Jointly with my partner,' she replied, staring at him. 'What the hell's up? Chaps of your rank wouldn't come round if someone reported Mrs Willis was fiddling the till.'

A nervous protest came from behind the counter.

'Murder is up,' Pollard replied briefly. 'We're working on the Redbay poisoning case, which you may have read about in the press. The cyanide which killed Mrs Audrey Vickers was contained in chocolates purporting to be made by this firm. I want them identified, if this is the case.'

'My—Gawd!' Zoë Morse exclaimed. 'What a prefectly bloody thing to happen! Or is it? I'm not so sure, come to that. Publicity—here, come into the store, will you,' she said hurriedly, as voices were heard outside the door. 'Not exactly a sales boost, is it?'

The store-room was lined with shelves, carrying what struck Pollard as surprisingly little stock. A businesslike desk had a telephone and a typewriter. The barred window overlooked a yard at the back of the house.

Zoë Morse sat down heavily behind the desk, still staring at Pollard who took the only other chair. Toye quietly occupied the vantage point of the window-sill.

'Well, you'd better let me look at the things, hadn't you?' she said.

Pollard glanced over his shoulder, and Toye came forward with a case which he put on the desk, and proceeded to unlock. Pollard took out a flat transparent plastic box containing half a dozen chocolates. It was sealed with adhesive tape, and marked 'poison'.

'Don't touch this, please, Mrs Morse,' he said authoritatively, putting the box on the blotter in front of her. 'Look carefully at the top of the chocolates, please and then I'll turn it over, so that you can see what they're like underneath.'

The chocolates were about an inch square, and half an inch thick. Each was surmounted by the letter M in a flowing script.

'Go ahead,' Zoë Morse said, after a brief inspection.

Pollard turned the box over, and handed her a lens.

'Look at them through this please,' he requested.

'They're our Marchpane Magic,' she said without hesitation. 'There's no doubt whatever. We dry our chocolates on patterned foil with a design of tiny skeps. See? It's our trade mark, so to speak. The break in the pattern's where the stuff was put in, I suppose? How on earth was it done?'

'Our experts report that a tiny shaft was drilled, possibly with the stem of a small funnel used in scientific work. A little column of the filling was lifted out, the cyanide put in, and the chocolate put on very gentle heat, again on foil, so that there would be slight melting, and the hole could be smeared over. Only the foil was the plain variety, instead of the kind you use.'

'Whoever did it was nifty with his or her fingers,' Zoë Morse commented, peering through the lens. 'The stuff must be pretty lethal.'

'It certainly is,' Pollard replied, picking up the box, and returning it to the case. 'One of these would be more than enough to put paid to anybody.'

She laughed shortly.

'Handy little things to have around. I could do with a few myself.'

Pollard realized that she was eyeing him with an interest unconnected with his professional activities. As her foot pressed his under the desk he moved his chair back with an abstracted air.

'Now we want you to look at the box the chocolates were sent in, and the packaging material inside it,' he said. 'You can handle it all freely. Our experts have made their examination.'

The colour and design of the box was exactly the same as that of the display box in the shop window. Zoë Morse slid off the cover and took out a sheet of semi-transparent waxed paper which had originally covered the chocolates. She held it up to the light.

'Ours, all right,' she said. 'It's got our perforated date stamp. See?'

'You mean,' Pollard asked, sharply alerted, 'that every box of your products carries a record of the date when they were made?'

'The date when they were packaged, actually.' She leant back, her dress straining provocatively across her breasts. 'There could be an overnight interval. Our goods are luxury class, Mr Superintendent Pollard, and pricey to match. So they have to be freshly made for our type of client. Surely you've noticed that we don't carry a big stock?'

'When were the chocolates we're discussing made?' he asked brusquely, ignoring her mocking expression.

'If they left our factory with this waxed paper, they were made early on Monday, April the thirtieth, and packaged that same afternoon. A week ago yesterday, that is. So glad to be helping the police with their enquiries.'

'It's much too early to say whether the information you're giving will be of any value or not. Assuming that the chocolates were sent here from the factory, when would they have been delivered?' Pollard tried to keep the interest he felt out of his voice.

'God, I don't know to the minute,' Zoë Morse replied irritably. 'They'd have come the next day, sometime in the morning. Mrs Willis might remember.'

Pollard glanced round at Toye.

'Ask Mrs Willis to come in here for a moment, Sergeant.'

Mrs Willis came in, darting anxious looks from one person to another.

'Perhaps you can help us over a matter of timing, Mrs Willis,' Pollard said. 'Just put your mind back to a weeek ago today. That would be Tuesday, May the first, wouldn't it? Can you remember when the delivery from the factory arrived?'

The colour drained out of her face, and she stared at him like a small frightened animal.

'What on earth are you looking like a stuck pig for?' Zoë Morse demanded impatiently. 'Can't you answer a perfectly simple question?'

'I'm conducting this interview, Mrs Morse,' Pollard interposed sharply. 'Take your time, Mrs Willis. I expect one delivery from the factory is very like another, isn't it?'

She looked at him gratefully.

'I can remember the time, sir, as it happens. The van was very late, and didn't get here till close on a quarter to one. Usually it's soon after twelve. Driver said the traffic jams were worse than ever that day.'

'Been in somewhere for a quick one,' interjected Zoë Morse.

'Thank you, Mrs Willis,' Pollard said. 'Now there's just one other thing. Would you take these photographs, and see if you can remember any of the people coming in and buying March-pane Magic chocolates on that Tuesday afternoon? Just do your best. Take them into the shop, and have a look.'

To his surprise she almost snatched them from his hand, and hurried out of the room.

'My God, what a fool that woman is,' Zoë Morse remarked. 'Mercifully she's honest, or I wouldn't keep her for five minutes. You have to take what you can get these days.'

Without comment Pollard embarked on a brisk enquiry into the organization of Honeydew. He learnt that there was a small factory in Hackney, and that the manufacturing side of the business was run by Zoë Morse's male partner, while she was responsible for sales. Post orders went out directly from the factory. Mrs Willis was merely in charge of shop sales on a salaried basis. The mere possibility of any of the factory staff being involved in the murder of Audrey Vickers was scoffed at.

'Better come down and grill 'em yourself,' Zoë Morse suggested. 'Then you can see what post orders went off,' she added persuasively. 'I'll run you down. Just give me ten minutes to square things up here.'

Avoiding Toye's eye, Pollard replied that a visit to the factory was next on their list.

'Could my sergeant use that typewriter?' he asked. 'If we can make out a summary of the information you've given us now for your signature, it will save everyone's time.'

'Make yourselves at home by all means,' she replied, vacating the desk and proceeding to file some letters.

Pollard found Mrs Willis handing a customer some purchases in a smart carrier bag patterned with Honeydew straw skeps. The photographs were neatly stacked on the counter. As soon as they were alone she picked them up and returned them. Rather to his surprise she volunteered a statement at once.

'I'm quite sure none of these young ladies came in that Tuesday afternoon, sir,' she said.

'How about a young man who looked like this?' he asked, and embarked on a detailed description of Keith Lang.

Her characteristic worried expression returned.

'I don't recollect anyone like that, either,' she said. 'after all, it's a week ago, and people coming in and out all the time.'

'Of course,' Pollard said reassuringly, and thanked her for her help. At the same time he had a depressing mental picture of her under cross-examination. Somehow or other they must get hold of a photograph of Keith Lang.

After some tiresome badinage Zoë Morse signed the statement prepared by Toye, and the trio left together. On the pavement outside Pollard raised his hat politely.

'Many thanks for giving Sergeant Toye a lift, Mrs Morse,' he said. 'He'll be making the enquiries at the factory, as I'm due elsewhere. Goodbye.'

He turned and made swiftly for West Audley Street, hugging himself, and only regretting the impossibility of being an invisible third in the car, to enjoy the imperturbable Toye's handling of the situation.

He sat in the car for a minute or two, assessing the facts gained from the Honeydew interviews. A *terminus a quo* for getting hold of the chocolates was a useful step forward. Obviously the Langs could have bought them on the Tuesday afternoon, but on the other hand, Mrs Willis's evidence—for what it was worth—looked like clearing Drusilla, and to some extent her husband. . . . A photograph of Keith Lang must be got hold of somehow. . . . What was wanted now was the sort of information about Donald Vickers which would either bring him into the picture or put him right out of it. . . .

At Odyssey Tours Pollard assured Mr Hedley, the managing director, that he had not come to go over the ground already covered by Sergeant Longman, and produced the compliments slip sent to Audrey Vickers with the chocolates. He learnt that the slip was enclosed in all tour brochures sent out from the office, not merely with those dealing with Odyssey cruises. Clients who made bookings got a second slip when their tickets were sent to them.

'The only thing of the slightest interest I can tell you about this particular specimen,' Mr Hedley said, examining it carefully, 'is that it's one of our most recent batch. I can tell by the slightly darker colour. That means it came into circulation last autumn—roughly when the programmes for this year were going out. I remember because of a hold-up at the printers: we thought we were going to run out of the old lot.'

Pollard asked him if there were any records of people who wrote for brochures.

'Oh, yes. We should contact them again the next year, whether they made a booking or not. Any names you'd like looked up?'

'Lang,' Pollard said. 'And Vickers, other than the late Mrs Audrey.'

There was an interval while this information was being sought, during which Mr Hedley showed a natural curiosity about the circumstances of Audrey Vickers' death, and Pollard tried to gratify this without telling him a great deal. Presently a member of the office staff came in with a paper in his hand.

'There are no Langs on this year's list, sir,' he told Mr Hedley, 'but a Mr D. J. Vickers wrote from Philadelphia last October, and afterwards booked for his wife and himself on the Egyptian tour in March. I've made a note of the address.'

'Any use to you?' the managing director asked, when the man had gone.

'Could be,' Pollard replied, suppressing his excitement as he carefully put away the address in his wallet.

'I hope I haven't stuck my neck out,' Mr Hedley went on, 'but when the cruise manager rang me about something from Rhodes last night, it seemed a chance to ask if anything in the least relevant to this business had got round to him. From a member of our staff on board, for instance. Nothing whatever, he said.'

'Even an answer of that sort's useful,' Pollard told him. 'At least one knows what not to spend time asking.'

A few minutes later he was on his way back to the Yard, convinced that news must have come in by now. He felt so certain of this that it was no surprise to be greeted by his secretary with two typewritten reports.

The first, from the British Embassy in Washington, stated that Donald James Vickers had acquired United States citizenship on 12 May, 1955, and had married Maria Grant Marella on 2 June 1955.

The second, from the Athens police, informed him that a Mr and Mrs D. J. Vickers, holders of valid US passports, had left Athens by air for Rome on the morning of Saturday, 28 April.

Pollard read both reports a second time with the sensation of being borne triumphantly aloft.

EIGHT

Summoned after lunch to report to the Assistant Commissioner, Pollard found him in an irascible mood, suffering from a streaming cold in the head. A copy of the Vickers file was lying on his desk.

'I've waded through this,' he said, pushing it impatiently aside. 'Looks a straightforward case to me. I can't see any sound reason for not pulling in the niece and the husband.'

'It's partly that there doesn't seem to be a convincing motive, sir, and partly because they both seem far too intelligent to embark on such a very obvious crime,' Pollard replied, forbearing to add that this information was clearly set out in the file.

The AC snatched a man-sized paper handkerchief from a box, and blew his nose with a couple of resounding blasts, between which Pollard caught a four-letter word.

'Motive! Last thing you want to bother about. Means and opportunity are the things to go for. I should have thought you'd have found that out for yourself, if they forgot to mention it in the training course. As to intelligence—my foot! Everybody knows that however bright the young are, they've absolutely no powers of self-criticism. Never occurs to 'em how the things they do strike other people.'

'I absolutely agree, sir,' Pollard said diplomatically. 'But the fact is that it's now a probability that Audrey Vickers and her bigamous husband collided head-on in Athens, and if they did, they could hardly have helped recognizing each other. Some more facts have just come in about Vickers. He's become a pretty warm chap—owns a motel chain in the States, and another in Canada. He'd have a lot to lose from exposure, even if bigamy isn't an extraditable offence in his case.'

An explosive sneeze was the AC's immediate response. As he blew his nose again he remarked indistinctly that even if it were, the Yard had something better to do with its time. He flung a second handkerchief into a wastepaper basket, and sat staring balefully at his subordinate.

'Look here, Bollard,' he began, sniffing violently. 'You've had some unusual cases with freak solutions. Fair enough. I don't say you haven't handled 'em well, but it's god you idto the way of shying off the obvious. Dangerous habid. This Vickers fellow. Eben if he did cub on here, where in hell did he ged the cyadide? Tell me thad.'

All too conscious of being driven on to the defensive, Pollard replied that he had some possible lines of enquiry in mind. The AC countered with a demand to know what arrangements had been made for keeping the Langs under observation. On hearing that Pollard had not thought continuous shadowing necessary, he exploded again.

'If they gib you the slib, it's your respodsibility,' he concluded. 'Ad thad's all I've god to say. I oughdn't to be here. I'b goig hobe to bed: odly thig to do with a bloody code like this,' he added, with the pettishness of a healthy male afflicted by a minor ailment.

Pollard thankfully escaped. As he went through the outer office, he exchanged raised eyebrows and despairing looks with the AC's secretary.

After this depressing encounter Toye's enthusiasm about the report from Washington was gratifying. A careful worker to the point of over-conscientiousness, Toye was sometimes alarmed by Pollard's flashes of inspiration, but always full of generous admiration when they came off. They settled down to plan a course of action in the event of news coming through from Rome that the Donald Vickers had flown on to London. Their arrival at Heathrow or Gatwick would have to be verified, and enquiries made at the likely hotels....

'And if they didn't turn up here after all,' Pollard said, with rather elaborate casualness, 'well, that's that. Now then, how did you get on down at that factory? Enjoy the drive?'

The lady, Toye told him, had been properly put out. Face like thunder, and took it out of the car. Shocking driving. It was a wonder they hadn't had a crash the way she'd jumped the lights and overtaken. Never spoke a word till they got there, bar cursing other drivers. Then she'd chucked him at her partner's head and disappeared.

Pollard grinned.

'Anything useful there?' he asked.

'He was quite a different cup of tea, sir. Interested, and keen to help. He got the names and addresses of the people whose post orders went off that Tuesday typed out for me. Then I asked about the factory staff. It's quite a small concern, and the way they've got things fixed only half a dozen could have snitched a box of the chocolates with all the trimmings, and that's including the two partners. I had a word with the other four, and I'd

93

say it's a million to one against them being mixed up in the business. I took their names, of course.'

'Let's have a look at those post orders,' Pollard said.

It was a fairly long list of varied orders, but only ten customers had asked for Marchpane Magic. None of them was called Lang or Vickers, and none lived at Fulminster. A further check showed that with the possible exception of a Mrs Brown of Newcastle-upon-Tyne, none of the *Penelope*'s passengers appeared to have ordered Honeydew products to be despatched on Tuesday, 1 May.

'It probably isn't the same Brown, anyway,' Pollard said, 'and the time posts take would rule her out, anyway. I never expected much from this. It would be so much simpler to shove on a false beard or a pair of sun glasses, and buy the Marchpanes over the counter. Much safer, too, than putting an order on paper. What's on your mind?'

'I've been wondering, sir,' Toye replied slowly, 'how Donald Vickers—if he's our chap—found out that Mrs V was on the *Penelope*?'

'I've thought about that one myself,' Pollard said. 'I think he must have heard her demanding to be taken back to the ship. According to Mrs Strode the American party went on nattering, and Mrs V subsided on to a chunk of masonry quite close. He'd realize that she almost certainly didn't mean the American cruise ship, which I expect the people he was talking to hailed from. And an enterprising chap like Vickers could easily find out what British cruise was in, and ring the ship, asking if a Mr and Mrs XYZ Vickers were on board. The ship's telephonist would say no, but there was a Mrs Audrey Vickers, and did he possibly mean her?'

Toye, a little doubtfully, agreed that this was a possible explanation.

'You know, I don't think finding out where she lived would have been much of a poser to the chap,' Pollard went on. 'They had their honeymoon at Redbay, remember, and Audrey Vickers went there after her husband had faded out. We don't know that he never turned up at all after the war. They could have tried to make a go of it, and even discussed a divorce before he decided that it would be a lot simpler to clear off. She might have said that she would go and live in Redbay. Nothing would have been simpler than looking her up in a Highcastle area telephone directory when he got to London. . . . Always assuming he did, of course. . . . What the hell are those chaps in Rome doing? I know I'm theorizing madly. Look here, we ought to be pushing off to Thrale, Keith Lang's publisher. It struck me that since they've taken on his novel, they may have asked him for a photograph to stick on the back of the jacket. And his alleged visit there last Thursday must be checked, anyway.'

When they returned two hours later, there was still no report from Rome on the Donald Vickers' movements.

'We may as well pack it in for today,' Pollard said. 'Take this along before you go, though, and ask 'em to blow it up.'

He stared for a moment at the passport photograph which Keith Lang had given to his publishers, and then passed it over to Toye.

When the latter had gone Pollard sat down at his desk to digest the day's developments in solitude. He had an excellent visual memory, and soon one interview after another began to pass before his mind like pictures on a television screen. . . . Toye sitting over there early on, at that stage politely and unmistakably sceptical about Donald Vickers. Not to be wondered at, come to that. Pollard conceded. That chance meeting on the Acropolis took a bit of swallowing, and even now it wasn't proven. But was it any more fantastic than coincidences which had cropped up in other cases, pointing the way to totally unexpected solutions?

Toye's familiar face faded out, and was replaced by Mrs Willis's, her eyes peering out anxiously from under her fringe, her background the lush Honeydew set-up. Why on earth did she stay in the job to be bullied by that cow Zoë Morse? There were endless openings for saleswomen in London, and it wasn't likely that a small show like Honeydew paid outstandingly well. Could it be that Zoë Morse had some hold over her? Pollard decided that this was a possibility, but one with no obvious bearing on this case. . . . Now Mrs Willis was looking at him quite confidently, and saying that she was sure none of the originals of the photographs had come into Honeydew's on the afternoon of Tuesday, 1 May. As he went on to describe Keith Lang the worried expression had returned to her face. . . .

Curious little thing, Mrs Willis. Apparently scared stiff of her employer but with a certain toughness and shrewdness underneath. Perhaps the integrity which Morse had contemptuously recognized gave her a kind of last ditch confidence.

He'd have to see her again with the blown-up photograph, of course. Unless things started happening in a big way over Donald Vickers ...

Some unexpected brief shots of events on the vital Tuesday, just a week ago, presented themselves. The arrival lounge at Heathrow: Audrey Vickers pointedly dissociating herself from the Langs, following a porter with a luggage barrow to a taxi, getting in fussily and telling the cabby to drive to Waterloo.... Back to the Langs, humping their baggage to the airport bus, arriving at the air terminal.

The sequence of pictures broke at this point, and efforts to visualize Keith arriving in Market Court en route for Honeydew failed. Instead there came a flash of two figues dwarfed by the portico of the British Museum.

Vaguely disturbed, Pollard opened his eyes, and let them rest on the familiar surroundings of his room. Could it be, after all, that he was being pig-headed over the Langs, relying on his personal impressions rather than on facts? Closing them again he got a fleeting glimpse of the Assistant Commissioner's contorted pre-sneeze countenance. It was instantly replaced by the face of Rex Purcell, the Thrale editor who was dealing with Keith Lang's novel. An unusual face: rectangular, with a little slit of a mouth, and crowned by a bald dome encircled by a tatty fringe of hair, just as though the chap had an overdone tonsure. Very intelligent eyes looked out at him, as Purcell said how dicey launching unknown authors was these days. Young Lang had got something, though, he'd gone on to say. Sensitivity, for one thing, and the ability to criticize himself and his generation as well as the Establishment, finding the same weaknesses in both in different forms. With luck—and there was the hell of a lot of luck in it—he might make the grade.

Just what the AC said the young could never do, Pollard thought, harking back to Keith Lang's alleged capacity to see himself as others saw him. Was it after all possible that the intelligent couple had worked it out, and banked on the crime being considered too blatantly obvious for people with IQs like theirs? And then devoted their very considerable grey matter to covering their tracks?

He was assailed by these and other uncomfortable doubts. Then he saw once again the typescript of the report from Washington on Donald Vickers' naturalization ... the report from Athens about his departure for Rome on 28 April.

If only something would come in from Rome, he thought. . . .

Pollard roused himself abruptly. It was no use hanging around waiting for things to happen: it simply made one edgy. Much better to go home. Brightening at the prospect, he began to cram papers into his brief-case. Five minutes later he was unlocking his car, having left instructions for any reports to be telephoned to his home.

Jane opened the front door before he got his latchkey into the lock.

'The Yard's just rung through,' she told him. 'A Mr and Mrs Donald J. Vickers left Rome for London at eight-thirty am on Tuesday, 1 May, by an Alitalia flight.'

They looked at each other.

'There's nothing conclusive about this, you know,' Pollard said.

'But nothing to do with Donald Vickers could ever be conclusive without this particular link in the chain,' she argued. 'How about a drink before supper? Something else has come through, by the way. Andrew's molar!'

On the following morning Pollard woke with an urgent sense of importance of the day ahead. It hung over him as he ate an early breakfast, try though he might to appear his normal relaxed self. Jane, too perceptive to be solicitous, supplied him briskly with food, and occupied herself in getting the twins dressed. With a great effort she refrained from squeezing her husband's hand as he kissed her goodbye rather absently before setting out.

On arriving at the Yard Pollard found that enquiries at Heathrow were already in progress. Keith Lang's photograph had been successfully blown up, and was lying on his desk. There *is* a kind of maturity about the chap, he thought, studying it carefully. His hangover from adolescence is that touch of gaucheness when you talk to him. . . .

'I'll just nip along to Honeydew with this one, and two or three more like it,' he said to Toye. 'It won't take long, and gets another point checked. No need for you to come as well. I think Mrs Willis might be more oncoming with only one of us around.'

When he arrived at Number Seven Market Court, the step was newly washed and the brass knocker and letter-box shone like gold. He hesitated for a moment, but decided to stick to his usual technique of playing it by ear. On walking into the shop he found Mrs Willis whisking a feather duster over a display stand. Swift as lightning he cashed in on what the AC had once called his personable quality.

'Me again, dear,' he said. 'Just another bit of red tape to tidy up. I don't hear a kettle on the boil in there, do I? Could there be a cuppa going? It's the whale of a long time since I had breakfast.'

As Pollard had almost unconsciously hoped, this opening conjured up a cosy conspiratorial atmosphere as if by magic. Mrs Willis, at first taken aback, responded with a smile.

'I don't know what Mrs Morse would say,' she parried.

'Don't you?' he replied, grinning broadly. 'Perhaps I'd better not tell a lady, though.'

'In here, then,' she said, leading the way to the stock room. 'There's not many come in before eleven, and Mrs Morse isn't one for early hours.'

'Late hours, more like?' Pollard suggested, installing himself at the desk. Mrs Willis darted an expressive glance at him as she filled the teapot, but made no comment.

The tea was good, boiling hot and not too strong. He gulped appreciatively and set down his half-empty cup.

'Ah, that's better,' he said. 'Well, now, it's this Redbay case again. It's giving us the heck of a lot of bother. I mustn't go around shooting my mouth, but there's no harm in telling someone like you that we're very interested in two people at the moment. It was three until you crossed one off the list for us yesterday.'

The remark clearly made her uneasy. She made no reply, and sat staring at her teacup.

'I've brought along another batch of photographs,' he went on chattily, reaching for his brief-case. 'Big ones. They've been blown up—enlarged—from smaller ones. Half a dozen young men for you this time. Take a good look for me, dear, and see if any of 'em rings a bell.'

As Mrs Willis took the photographs from him he saw that her hand shook slightly. She dropped them on to the table.

'I don't like this sort of thing,' she protested tremulously. 'It's—it's too much responsibility. Not reasonable, either. With customers coming and going all the time, how can you remember what they all looked like? The police shouldn't expect it.

'The police never expect anything,' Pollard said easily, 'but

98

we have to go on trying our luck, you know. Just have a go, that's all, I shan't press you to pick anyone out.'

Reluctantly she began to look through the photographs, giving a reasonable time to each, but Pollard felt convinced that she was not really giving them her attention. He watched her, puzzled and intrigued by her behaviour. She came to the last one, scrutinized it briefly, and then swept them all together with an impulsive movement.

'None of this lot came in that afternoon, either,' she said, hurriedly and emphatically.

'Are you absolutely sure, Mrs Willis?' Pollard asked gently. 'You said just now how difficult it was to remember with all the comings and goings.'

'You know quite well who you haven't seen,' she replied rather wildly, now fixing her gaze on the yard beyond the barred window.

'Well, well, there's another possible lead gone west,' he commented philosophically, restoring the photographs to his briefcase.

Unexpectedly Mrs Willis broke the silence by offering him another cup of tea. Pollard accepted, his interest alerted. Could it be that she was going to talk? He now felt quite certain that something off-beat was going on at Honeydew. He tried to reduce tension by talking about the business, and enquiring into prices.

'If your stuff isn't too ruinous I'd like to take my wife something,' he told her.

Instantly full of bright interest Mrs Willis sprang to her feet and went to the shelves. Several boxes were brought for his inspection, and he finally settled for a costly pound of Fudge Favourites.

What a fool I am, he thought, following her into the shop. The moment she was back on her own ground she felt confident again, and shut up like a clam. All I can do now is drop a hint about this place in the right quarter. . . .

'Now I'll have to dash off,' he said, accepting his change and purchase. 'Thanks so much for the char, dear, and for having a look at those lads. If you happen to think of anything at all that might help, give me a ring, won't you? Here's my card. Just dial that number, and ask for me. Any time.'

Pollard had hardly left the shop when the whole interview dropped out of his mind, as an urgent desire to get back to the

Yard possessed him. Picking up the Donald Vickers trail at Heathrow couldn't conceivably take as long as tracing them in Rome, he thought, getting into his car. News of some sort would surely have arrived by now.

Automatically negotiating the stop-go of the traffic lights, he alternated between exhilaration and depressing awareness of problems yet to be solved. It was a coup to have got on to Donald Vickers at all. But that damned cyanide was the thing. . . . If he didn't arrive in England until Tuesday, surely he must have got hold of the stuff in Italy. What sort of poison laws did they have over there? Owning a chain of motels didn't seem likely to give you the entrée to farms or factories where the stuff might be around. Wait a bit. . . . He changed gear badly while delving into his memory. Yes, Vickers had 'married' an American girl with an Italian name. They might have linked up with her people in Italy . . . farmers, perhaps. Rather a wild idea, but it could be worth following up. Family relationships counted for a lot among Italians. . . .

Tenuous though the idea certainly was, Pollard arrived at the Yard with optimism in the ascendant. Rather than wait for a lift he took the stairs two at a time.

His secretary and Toye were standing together in the middle of the room as he came in. They turned quickly. There was a fractional silence.

'Well?' he demanded.

'Report from Heathrow, sir,' Toye told him unhappily. 'A Mr and Mrs Donald Vickers landed from Rome at ten twenty-nine am on Tuesday, 1 May. They were in transit, and left again for New York by a BOAC flight at eleven-fifty the same morning.'

Pollard had a sensation of being precipitated into a totally different context. Before he could rally himself he was astonished by an outburst from Toye.

'It's cruel,' the latter exploded, his normally impassive face red. 'A super stroke of yours, sir, tracking Vickers down. Not one in hundreds could've pulled it off. And to think the bleeder's in the clear, seeing he'd taken off before the ruddy chocolates were on sale!'

Pollard stared at him, absurdly moved.

'Come on, old cock,' he said. 'Here we are back in that well-known spot Square One. We'd better take stock, hadn't we?'

Surrounded by a litter of sandwich crumbs, ash trays, typescript and jottings on slips of paper, Pollard and Toye concen-
trated fiercely on the Vickers file. In the companionable atmosphere of shared disappointment they worked for the most part
in silence, only occasionally raising brief queries. It was mid-
afternoon when they surfaced and pooled their findings. Cast in
its final form, the list was meagre.

Possible Fresh Leads
1 Fingerprint of small child on cellophane wrapping of box of
Marchpane Magic.
2 Odd reactions of Mrs Willis when asked to identify Honeydew customers from photographs.
3 The name Bayley keeps cropping up. Picture at Lauriston
signed J. Bayley. A Mr and Mrs John Bayley on the cruise.
House belonging to the latter destroyed as result of arson
during the period of the cruise.

Pollard threw down his pen.

'Well, we've scraped the barrel,' he said. 'So what? I'll tell
you. Either we justify work on one or more of these leads
pronto, or it's a warrant for the Langs. The AC'll be back tomorrow: he's only got a stinking cold in the head. Let's take
them in turn. What about the kid?'

'There could've been one at the factory or the shop,' Toye
replied doubtfully. 'From what I saw of it, I'd be inclined to
rule out the factory. How about a customer's kid running
around at the shop, and grabbing at the stuff on the display
stands? Then the murderer comes along, and buys a box of
Marchpane Magic the kid's fingered.'

'It's an idea,' Pollard allowed. 'It means getting Willis to talk.
At the moment she's too scared about something to open her
mouth. Probably nothing relevant to the case. We might go
along and take a tougher line with her. Tackle Leads One and
Two at the same time, in fact.

He broke off to make a note.

'What about Lead Three? If you can call it a lead, that is.'

There was silence in the room for a few moments.

'We don't know for a fact that the John Bayley on the cruise

101

didn't paint that picture,' Toye remarked. 'We've only Mrs Lang's word for it that he said he hadn't, come to that.'

'True,' Pollard replied. 'The same thought's just hit me. I can't see any reason why Mrs Lang should have lied about it, but it's easy to understand why John Bayley might have. Wouldn't you have gone to almost any length to escape getting involved with Mrs Vickers on a cruise ship? I know I would. Mrs Strode said she'd never seen the chap painting during the trip, but that could mean he'd decided it wasn't worth the sweat of bringing his painting gear.'

Toye agreed that all this was fair enough.

'That arson business, sir. I suppose it can't possibly tie up with our case?'

Pollard sat frowning and doodling on his blotter.

'I don't see how it possibly can,' he said at last. 'To begin with, there's absolutely no doubt that both the Bayleys were on the ship when the fire took place. Unless they had an accomplice, with all the risk of blackmail this would involve, how could they have had a hand in it? Even if we assume for purposes of argument that they had, I just can't swallow the theory that Audrey Vickers managed to find out, and they decided to murder her to shut her mouth. Even wilder than my Donald Vickers theory, what?'

'It wasn't all that wild,' Toye insisted loyally. 'Why, the chap *was* Donald Vickers. At least, Vickers must have been in Athens when she was there, and he's her lawful husband into the bargain.'

Pollard stretched slowly, and clasped his hands behind his head.

'Well,' he said without enthusiasm, 'I suppose we'd better make tracks for Honeydew, and grill Mrs Willis.... Hold on, though. I've just had a nasty thought that the place is shut on Wednesday afternoons. There was a notice about hours on the door. Ring through, will you? If she answers, you can say you've got the wrong number, or something.'

Toye made two attempts to get Honeydew without success.

'Seems you're right,' he said.

Pollard grunted and sat staring in front of him for several moments.

'That water-colour at Lauriston,' he said abruptly. 'There was a framer's label on the back. A Redbay chap with a comic name ... wait a bit ... I've got it. Batholomew Popkiss. Audrey

102

Vickers was a compulsive talker, wasn't she? It's just on the cards that she said something to Popkiss about J. Bayley. Let's see if we can get on to him.'

After an interval Toye reported that the number had been found.

'Bet it's early closing in Redbay, too,' Pollard observed gloomily, picking up the receiver of his desk telephone.

'You're through,' said a voice.

'Mr Popkiss?' he queried, sounding surprised. 'Good afternoon. Detective-Superintendent Pollard speaking from New Scotland Yard. You may have heard of me. I'm conducting the enquiry into the death of Mrs Audrey Vickers.'

There were sounds of elderly agitation.

'Nothing to worry about, Mr Popkiss. There's just a small matter you may be able to clear up for us. Mrs Vickers was a customer of yours, I think?'

Now on the familiar ground of his business the picture-framer became more coherent. Yes, he'd done jobs for the poor lady from time to time.

'Do you remember framing a water-colour of a famous bridge in Florence for her, a few years ago? It's called the Ponte Vecchio, and the picture's signed J. Bayley.'

Mr Popkiss replied without hesitation that he remembered it well. There had been a lot of photos of the bridge in the papers when they had the bad floods in Italy, and he'd recognized it as the one he'd framed for Mrs Vickers.

'Did she tell you anything about the artist? Where he lived, for instance?'

'Not to tell me anything, she didn't, but now you come to mention him, I call to mind there was a little printed label stuck on the back of the picture, down at the bottom left-hand corner with his name and address on it. But I don't remember the address, not after all this time.'

'It's surprising you even remember the label, considering all the pictures you must handle,' Pollard told him tactfully. 'It was left on the back of the water-colour, I take it?'

To his relief, it had been, and after thanking Mr Popkiss for his help, he rang off, and turned to Toye.

'Come on,' he said. 'I know it's a hundred to one that we're heading for a dead end, but anything's better than just sitting around on our backsides. The keys of Lauriston are at the Redbay station. Let's see if we can contact Inspector Morris, and get him to go along and open up that frame.'

By a stroke of good luck Inspector Morris was available, and sounded pleased at a request for help from the Yard. He undertook to go to Lauriston at once, and ring back with the address.

'Now for the address of the cruise Bayleys,' Pollard remarked, trying to suppress a feeling of excitement which seemed to him quite unjustified. 'Dart—no, Odyssey Tours, of course. Cheaper call for the taxpayer to foot.'

This time he handled the call himself, and was put through to Mr Hedley.

'Easy,' replied the latter, on hearing what was wanted. 'Hang on a few minutes, and I'll have the address looked up for you right away.'

He was as good as his word, and soon back on the line.

'Ready to take it down?' he enquired. 'Here goes. Mr and Mrs John Bayley, Ten Trafalgar Terrace, Camden Town, London NW1. Got it?'

'Thanks very much. I'll read it back . . .'

'Always glad to help the police. Mustn't ask how you're getting on, I suppose?'

'Sure you may. We've a handy stock answer: the police are continuing their enquiries.'

They concluded the call on the best of terms.

'Inspector Morris is the slow but sure type,' Pollard remarked, looking at his watch. 'We shan't hear anything from him for half an hour at least. I'd better tackle the In tray while we're waiting.'

In the event it was forty minutes before the switchboard operator announced that Redbay station wanted Superintendent Pollard. Inspector Morris reported back with exasperating deliberation.

'The printed label,' he concluded, 'measuring approximately one inch by one inch and a half, is affixed to the bottom left-hand corner. It bears the following inscription: J. Bayley, Ten Trafalgar Terrace, Camden Town, London NW1. I made a temporary repair to the frame, and rehung the picture pending your further instructions.'

Pollard thanked him, and rang off as soon as he decently could. He found Toye, who had been listening in at the extension, looking at him with admiration on his normally impassive face.

'I'll hand it to you, sir,' he remarked.

'Don't let's kid ourselves that we've got anywhere, though, old chap. If it turns out that John Bayley really is J. Bayley, and lied to Audrey Vickers in self-defence, we're no further on. If by any chance there's another J. Bayley living at the Trafalgar Terrace address, he might possibly be worth following up. We'll go along there now, on chance. Better not to alert them by ringing first. I think the best line to take is that we assume the two J.B.s are the same chap. Hence our call. We wonder if by any chance he knew the late Mrs Vickers, etc, etc. Then, if it turns out there are two chaps, we ask if the non-cruise one is in, because we'd just like a word with him. Play it by ear, of course. Not like me to plan an approach like this, is it? But we're going to sound a bit thin, let's face it.'

'Won't they think it's a bit odd that we haven't discussed it all with the Langs?' Toye asked. 'After all, they would know if Mrs Vickers had seen much of the Bayleys.'

'That's certainly a point,' Pollard agreed. 'If it strikes them, they'll probably conclude that we're checking up on the Langs' statements. I'm quite sure popular opinion has cast the Langs as the obvious suspects in the case. Harking back to the fire, I shan't mention it. The Bayleys may, of course, and we'll watch out for anything that might be useful to Dart. Let's find out now if the local lads know anything of interest about the Bayleys, and then we'll go and have some grub before we start off.'

A telephone call produced the information that as far as the local police were concerned, the Bayleys of Ten Trafalgar Terrace, were in the clear, even where motoring offences were concerned. Would Superintendent Pollard like any enquiries made?

Pollard explained that he was at the early stages of a doubtful lead, but might be glad of some help later. If so, he'd get into touch. He rang off with thanks for the offer, and turned to Toye.

'I rather fancy a preliminary snoop round on our own,' he said. 'We might drop into a shop, or a pub for a quick one when they open. It's no good getting to the house until John Bayley's had reasonable time to come home from his job.'

This programme was duly carried out. The car journey was slow in the heavy northbound traffic of the late afternoon, in spite of Toye's skilful diversions among the network of side-roads beyond Portland Place. Eventually they arrived in the neighbourhood of Trafalgar Terrace, and succeeded in parking. Pollard, who had had plenty of time to meditate on the probable uselessness of the trip, and the wisdom of his handling of the case, looked about him rather gloomily.

'Extraordinary hotchpotch,' he remarked. 'I can't see people knowing much about each other. Look at these Regency houses on the up and up, after going to seed before the war. Taken over by the new young-prosperous, and cheek by jowl with pricey little shops and chain stores and genuine working-class streets. Here's Trafalgar Terrace.'

They walked its full length, unobtrusively taking in the decorous three-storied houses with their pleasing proportions and good windows. The majority had obviously been carefully restored and modernized, and the row had a moneyed appearance. One house was enveloped in scaffolding, and in actual process of renovation. As they passed Number Ten Toye remarked that it had been given the full treatment.

'It's early yet,' Pollard said. 'Let's have a look at them from the back if it's possible.'

Investigation showed that the Trafalgar Terrace houses had small gardens at the back without separate access from the road, and joining on to the larger gardens of detached houses in Trafalgar Drive. Through a gap between two of the latter, they could see a single-storey building in the Bayleys' garden.

'Can't be a garage,' Toye said. 'There's no road.'

Pollard suddenly felt an inexplicable stir of excitement.

'Could be a studio,' he replied. 'I can't make out if it's got a north light, though.'

At the far end of Trafalgar Drive they came out again into the busy thoroughfare at right angles to the two roads of Regency houses, which contained a number of shops. He glanced critically at Toye.

'We might have a bash at that newsagent's,' he said. 'Try to look brisk and pursuing, and a bit as though you've had a busy day. You're an insurance chap, wanting Mr John Bayley. You've got an appointment and are muddled about Trafalgar Terrace and Trafalgar Drive. Get me?'

Commenting that play-acting wasn't really up his street, Toye adjusted his collar and jacket buttons, ran a hand through his sleek hair, and dived into the little shop, brief-case under his arm. In a couple of minutes he emerged again, and joined Pollard, who was studying the window of a delicatessen.

'Not much luck,' he announced. 'One of those women who talk to you with their minds on something else. But the Bayleys get their papers there, and buying that I thought I was late, I got out of her that he gets back from the place he works at about now, and that it's up near the North Circular somewhere.'

'Posh,' Pollard remarked a few minutes later, as they paused to admire a Jaguar Mark IV outside Number Ten, Trafalgar Terrace. 'He's back, anyway.'

After waiting briefly for Toye, a car enthusiast, to gloat, he rang the bell.

'Here goes,' he said.

The door was opened by a tall blonde with a kind of lacquered perfection about every detail of her appearance. She looked at him enquiringly without speaking.

'Good evening,' Pollard said. 'Mrs John Bayley?'

She replied briefly in the affirmative, conveying the impression that he had been weighed in the balance and found wanting.

'We're CID officers from New Scotland Yard, Mrs Bayley,' he told her. 'Detective-Superintendent Pollard, and Detective-Sergeant Toye. May we have a word with you and your husband?'

The pupils of her rather hard green eyes narrowed, and an exasperated expression came over her face.

'You can't mean this blasted business about the fire has got to Scotland Yard level?' she exclaimed. 'You'd better come in.'

Without waiting for an answer she led the way to an open door at the rear of the hall, through which a news broadcast was audible. Following her, Pollard caught a waft of an expensive perfume. A man was sprawled in an armchair by the open french window giving on to the garden, a half-empty tumbler on a small table at his side. As his wife came in he turned his head and stared.

'Scotland Yard,' she announced loudly and laconically, going over to the television set and switching it off. 'Detective-Superintendent Pollard and Detective-Sergeant . . .?'

'Toye,' Pollard supplied.

'Thanks. My husband, John Bayley,' she added.

The man, also tall and fair, struggled to his feet. Pollard placed him in his late thirties or early forties.

'Evening,' he said. 'I suppose we'll get to the end of this

107

confounded affair some day. Sit down, won't you? Any use offering you a drink?'

'I'm afraid not, as we're on duty,' Pollard told him, taking the chair indicated. 'Thanks all the same, though. I'd better say at once that I'm not with you about the fire Mrs Bayley mentioned just now. We've come along about something quite different.'

In the background a soda-water siphon gave an explosive splutter.

'Damn!' Mrs Bayley joined them, mopping herself with a handkerchief. 'Well, it'll be a change.' She sat down between Pollard and her husband.

'It certainly will,' the latter agreed, throwing himself back in his chair, and crossing his legs, while staring at Pollard with interest. 'Let's hear what it's in aid of, then.'

'We're probably wasting your time as well as our own,' Pollard replied, 'so I'll be as brief as possible. You've recently been on a Mediterranean cruise with Odyssey Tours, I understand?'

As he paused, both Bayleys made acquiescent noises while registering astonishment.

'In that case,' Pollard went on, 'no doubt you've read in the papers of the death of a fellow passenger, a Mrs Audrey Vickers, from eating poisoned chocolates sent to her through the post?'

'Why, yes,' Mrs Bayley said. 'We were staggered. We keep coming back to it, don't we John?'

'I don't quite see how we come in, though,' replied her husband.

'You probably don't come in at all, Mr Bayley,' Pollard told him. 'I'll explain. There are some odd features about the case which you'll understand I can't discuss at the moment. One line we're working on is to contact people Mrs Vickers may have talked to recently, possibly mentioning fears for her safety. We found a water-colour in her house signed J. Bayley, and his address, which was this house. As there were also a Mr and Mrs John Bayley on the cruise, again with this address, we wondered whether you and he were the same person, and might have known Mrs Vickers.'

Illumination spread over the two faces regarding him attentively.

'I get you,' John Bayley said, 'but I'm afraid you've been led up the Garden path, just as Mrs Vickers herself was. She accused me of painting the thing one day during the cruise, didn't she, Lorna? J. Bayley who paints is my cousin James Bayley. My brother-in-law, too, incidentally. My wife and I are cousins, you see. James and my having the same initial is a darned nuisance. We often have muddles over letters and bills, and so on.'

'Oh, well, that's one point cleared up, anyway,' Pollard said, a note of resignation in his voice. 'Can I have a word with Mr James Bayley, then, in case he can tell me anything about Mrs Vickers?'

'By all means, if you can run him to earth,' Mrs Bayley replied. 'I'm afraid we haven't a clue about where he is at the present moment.'

'But doesn't he live here, then?'

'Not in the usual sense,' John Bayley said. 'We've given him a couple of rooms on the top floor as a pied-à-terre, and he uses the studio out there when he's around, but he only turns up at intervals. The rest of the time he roams about abroad, painting when he feels like it. In Italy mostly, wouldn't you say, Lorna?'

'Mostly,' she agreed. 'I sometimes think my brother cultivates the popular image of an artist. He's casual and lazy, unless he's got a working fit on, and as he's got a little money he can afford this footloose thing. He's a good painter, though.'

'I could see that from Mrs Vickers' water-colour,' Pollard replied, amused as always to see the public's reaction to a policeman's interest in art. 'We may feel we want to contact him, though. When was he here last?'

'While we were on the cruise,' John Bayley replied, getting up to fetch himself another drink. 'I can't tell you the exact date, as our Mrs Mop doesn't come in when we're away. James can never be bothered to keep in touch, so there was no means of letting him know we were going on holiday. We just left a note on the mantelpiece on chance.'

'Which was just as well,' Lorna Bayley added, 'seeing that he wanted to see us about lending his rooms here to a pal.'

Under her half-flippant references to her brother Pollard thought he could detect genuine feeling. She's fond of the chap, he thought, hard-boiled though she looks.

'Did Mr James Bayley wait here until you came home?' he asked.

John Bayley gave an amused snort as he returned to his chair.

'Much too rational for old James, that. We'd given him our dates and plans in the note, saying we were having a week in Venice after the cruise, so he thought he'd join us, and flew straight out again. He might have saved himself the trouble: we had to come back as soon as we docked, and only had a morning with him.'

Pollard made no comment on this change of plan.

'So you left Mr James Bayley in Venice?' he said. 'Didn't he give you any idea of what he intended to do, as the joint holiday had fallen through?'

'He said something about knocking up a few potboilers before pushing on,' Lorna replied, 'but whether he did or not is another matter. Sorry to seem so unhelpful, but my brother's that sort of chap. If we couldn't give him house-room here, we probably shouldn't set eyes on him for years at a time.'

This time the affection underlying her rather offhand tone was quite unmistakable. John Bayley shifted his position impatiently.

'To be practical,' he said, 'it's a million to one against James being able to remember Mrs Vickers at all, even if she bought the water-colour from him personally: he's hopelessly vague. She probably just picked it up at one of the art shops in Italy which put his stuff on sale, or possibly at the Domani Gallery over here.'

'I see,' Pollard said. 'It certainly doesn't sound very hopeful. One more question, and we'll remove ourselves. How did Mrs Vickers strike you as a person? I gather that you had some conversation with her about the water-colour.'

'She was quite frightful,' Lorna Bayley replied emphatically. 'The cruise blight, in fact. One of those excitable middle-aged women who buttonhole people and pour out torrents of voluble conversation about themselves. Her appearance was the signal for a general fade-out, wasn't it, John?'

'Yes,' agreed her husband. 'She was easily top of the unpopularity poll on board. Broad and long it was a very decent crowd.'

'There was a good deal of feeling about the way she behaved to her niece and the niece's husband,' Lorna went on. 'Telling the whole ship she was paying for them, and never letting them go off on their own—you know. In the end they cut loose one day, and there was the hell of a row, apparently. At any rate the party wasn't on speaking terms by the end of the trip. Not that

I'm making any insinuations, of course.'

'Well,' Pollard said, getting to his feet, 'I'm glad to have got the matter of the two J. Bayleys of this address cleared up. If you hear from Mr James Bayley, would you ring me at the Yard? Here's my card. It's just possible that we may want to contact him for the record.'

John Bayley also got up, with an air of having found the interview a somewhat pointless interruption.

'We'll do that thing,' he said, 'but it's unlikely to happen. James isn't the type one hears from: he just turns up without warning, and as he was over so recently, he probably won't materialize for a while.'

'I suppose this chap James Bayley really exists?' Toye propounded as they walked away from the house.

'That crossed my mind for a moment,' Pollard replied, 'but he exists all right. The mention of the Domani clinches it. John Bayley would never have mentioned that it sold James's pictures if this wasn't true. It can be checked up so easily. And what's more, James has got to be found. In my own mind I'm pretty sure that the three of them conspired to burn down that house at Roccombe, and that James was the active partner.'

He relapsed into an abstracted silence. As they arrived at the main road Toye asked if they were going to the police station.

'Car,' Pollard said, 'to sort things out a bit.'

When they were installed and had lit cigarettes, he expelled a mouthful of smoke and looked at Toye.

'Perfect set-up for the arson stunt, isn't it?' he remarked. 'The whole neighbourhood in a state of coming and going, and an artistic brother-in-law who behaves like the Cheshire Cat.'

'You wouldn't expect an artist chap to be what you might call dependable over a dicey thing like arson,' Toye said thoughtfully.

'In some ways, no. But on the other hand he might take to it more easily than a steady nine-till-five chap. Get a kick out of doing down the insurance people, too. Then being a combined brother-in-law and brother could make it a family affair, and reduce the blackmail hazard. But anyway, this is Dart's problem. We just pass on the facts. Let's face it, we're no nearer finding a possible link with Audrey Vickers.'

They smoked in silence for a few moments.

'While you were talking I picked up two bits of information

about the Bayleys,' Toye said. 'A whole lot of stuff had been chucked down on the settee where I parked myself. Mr Bayley's jacket, and his brief-case with a lot of papers sticking out of it, and that women's magazine called *Eyeful*. Mrs Bayley models for rag trade photographers. It was open at an advert. She was wearing a posh affair all slit down the sides with trousers under it.'

'She's got the figure for it all right,' Pollard allowed. 'Was it this month's *Eyeful*?'

'Yes. I had a look, thinking I'd take my wife a copy. She'd be interested that I'd met the lady.'

'It's an idea. Get one for me, will you? What was the other thing you found out?'

'There was a wad of business letters in the brief-case. I didn't like to risk mucking them about too much, but I gave a bit of a tug, and the top one was headed Harrison and Wynne, and the first line of the address was Wentworth Road.'

'Could be Bayley's firm. We'll check up on it for Dart. We seem to be doing a lot of that bloke's work for him, don't we? By the way, did you notice that there weren't any kid's photographs in that room of the Bayleys?'

'Yes, I did. There weren't any in the front room, either. I took a quick look when we passed it on the way to the one at the back.'

'Can't see the Bayleys as parents,' Pollard said, stubbing out his cigarette. 'Too keen on their own standard of living, don't you think? Which brings me to tomorrow's programme. If we're having a showdown with Mrs Willis, the earlier the better, before the Morse woman turns up. We'll go along first thing. There's nothing more to be done around here: let's head for home.'

TEN

Pollard and Jane had an early breakfast together on the following morning.

'Well, one of two things is bound to happen today,' he said, pushing his empty coffee cup across the table. 'Either we get something out of Mrs Willis, or I report nothing doing on any front, get a flea in my ear from the AC, ask for a warrant for the Langs, and Toye and I trek down to Fulminster this afternoon.'

Jane refilled the cup and passed it back to him.

'What could you get from Mrs Willis that would help?' she asked. 'Apart from a positive identification of the Langs, I mean?'

'This is it,' Pollard replied, taking the last piece of toast. 'If only I knew that, things would be so much easier. The trouble is that I can't hit on anything that really looks like linking up with Audrey Vickers. The kid's print, as Toye says, was probably made by a customer's brat on the rampage grabbing the boxes on the stands. I expect it happens every time a kid's taken into the shop. Imagine yourself shopping with the twins in tow in about a year from now.'

Jane Pollard shuddered.

'Listen,' she said, cocking an ear. 'I thought I heard a yell. . . . No, it seems to be all right. Assunta really manages them very well.'

Pollard crunched, swallowed and drained his cup of coffee.

'Time I was off,' he said. 'I'll just look in on them before I go.'

He was given an enthusiastic reception in the twins' room. Assunta, who was struggling to get Andrew into a small blue shirt, beamed up at him.

'Good morning!' she exclaimed. 'Ecco il babbo, bambini!'

'Dad-dad-dad,' shouted Andrew with determined insularity. Rose, already dressed, streaked across the floor on all fours with excited cries. Pollard picked her up and pretended to toss her into the air, returned her to earth again and repeated the procedure with his son.

'How—is—Luigi?' he asked Assunta, who bridled and raised her eyes to heaven.'

' 'E is—aw kay.'

Pollard laughed.

'Fine,' he said. 'Now I must go. Goodbye, all of you.'

He departed amid protesting sounds from the twins, and ran downstairs. Jane had opened the garage for him.

'If it's Fulminster this afternoon, I'll ring you,' he promised, kissing her and getting into the car. As he drove out of the gate he turned for a final wave, seized with distaste for the programme ahead of him.

On arriving in his room at the Yard he saw that the meticulous Toye had already placed a copy of *Eyeful* on his desk. He glanced at the price, and was examining a handful of coins taken from his trouser pocket when Toye himself appeared.

'Thanks for getting this thing,' he said, handing over a couple of coins. 'I'll just see if anything vital's turned up, and if not we'll go along right away, and have a bash at little Willis.'

Ten minutes later they set out.

'My third visit,' Pollard remarked, as they arrived in West Audley Street. 'My last, too, I'm pretty sure. You know, I can't see anything coming out of this.'

'Some sort of racket behind Mrs Willis looking like a scared rabbit?' queried Toye.

'That, yes. Could be we'll have something to pass on to the appropriate quarter. Passing on gen seems to be our line at the moment, doesn't it?'

It was barely five minutes past nine when they arrived at Honeydew. The shop was empty, and Mrs Willis came hurrying out of the stock room still wearing a coat. At the sight of Pollard and Toye she stopped dead in her tracks.

'Yes, we're back again, Mrs Willis,' Pollard said. 'The police never give up, you know. Let's come in here to talk, shall we?' he added, manoeuvring her back to the stock room.

With obvious unwillingness she allowed herself to be escorted to the chair drawn up to face the desk, at which Pollard installed himself. He sat looking at her thoughtfully. Then he opened the file and took out the photograph of the child's fingerprint taken and blown up by Constable Bragg of High-castle.

'You see this fingerprint, Mrs Willis?' he asked, showing it to her. 'It was made by a young child about three or four years old.'

He watched her give an uncontrollable start.

'This print's important,' he went on. 'It was made on the cellophane wrapping of the box of Marchpane Magic sent to Mrs Vickers. I can see that you know something about it. Wouldn't you be wiser to tell me how it got on to the box? You see, if you don't I shall have to take steps to find out which you may not like at all.'

'Not Mrs Morse,' she pleaded, staring at him.

'I don't know what it is you're so anxious to keep from Mrs Morse,' Pollard said, 'but I promise you that unless it's absolutely necessary she won't be told.'

Mrs Willis's eyes searched his face as if seeking reassurance.

'I know I didn't ought to've done it,' she burst out, choking back a sob, 'but I was that worried I didn't know which way to turn. It was my daughter being taken bad in the street and rushed off to hospital like that; only seven months gone, she was, and her husband'd gone off and left her for another woman ... they took her in an ambulance. . . .'

Patiently and gently Pollard unravelled the story. Mrs Willis's daughter had collapsed while out shopping on the morning of Tuesday, May the first, and an ambulance had been summoned by passers-by. A neighbour had rung Mrs Willis at Honeydew, and she in turn had contacted the hospital to be given grave news of her daughter's condition and told to come immediately. Feeling desperate, and knowing that Zoë Morse was safely in Paris she had taken the unprecedented step of closing the shop, after an agonizing wait for the delayed delivery from the factory to arrive. The moment the van had driven away again she had locked up and fled in search of a taxi.

At this point in the story the outer shop door could be heard opening, announcing the arrival of a customer. In a flash Mrs Willis braced herself, and the mask of the bright obliging saleswoman dropped over her face.

'Please excuse me,' she said hurriedly, and left the stock room almost at a run.

Pollard turned to Toye, who was perched on the window sill as before.

'This might be useful, I suppose,' he said. 'She'll remember when she opened the place again, and that narrows down the time when the Langs could have bought the blasted chocolates. Always assuming they did, of course.'

Toye assented.

'Real bitch of a woman, that Mrs Morse,' he added, with unusual vehemence.

Through the door into the shop came the voice of Mrs Willis counting out change for a five pound note, and wishing the customer good morning. After a brief pause she reappeared. Pollard rose politely and waited for her to sit down again. His courtesy seemed to fluster her, and he made a comment on salesmanship in an attempt to relieve tension.

'Well now,' he resumed, 'you went off to the hospital as soon as the van had gone. What time did you get back and open the shop again?'

Her face was a study in guilt.

'I—I didn't,' she said, avoiding his eye. 'I was in the hospital right up to eight o'clock in the evening. 'Twasn't till then they said Shirley was out of danger.'

In the intense silence which followed this statement Pollard found that he was holding his breath. Suddenly he became aware that Mrs Willis was looking at him.

'I want to get this absolutely clear,' he said, recovering himself. 'Do you mean that the shop was closed from roughly one o'clock on that Tuesday morning until the following morning, and that during that time no one could buy anything here?'

'That's right,' she said miserably. 'I know it was wrong, cheating Mrs Morse out of the whole afternoon's takings. When she sees the book . . .'

'You couldn't possibly have done anything else but shut down,' Pollard cut in, 'seeing that you're singlehanded here. And as Mrs Morse was in Paris you couldn't possibly have contacted her.'

'I could've rung the factory and asked for Mr Peters—that's Mrs Morse's partner. I was that fussed I acted silly, looking back on it. I'm scared to death she'll find out somehow, and give me the sack. I've got to earn all the more now, with my daughter going on National Assistance, and I just feel I can't face a new job at my age. I mightn't get one: it's all young girls and mini-skirts these days. And I couldn't do with a big place. It's quiet on my own here, and a nice class of customer.'

Pollard did his best to be reassuring, and at last managed to bring Mrs Willis back to the subject of the fingerprint.

'It was my little granddaughter must've done it,' she told him, wiping her eyes. 'My sister over at Wallington said she'd take her while my daughter was in the hospital, me being out at work all day, but she couldn't come to fetch her before I left home. So I said I'd bring Tracy along here, only she must come as soon as she could. There was the Tuesday delivery to unpack and check, and it wouldn't do for customers to see the child about. I tried to keep the little thing in the stock room here, but I was in and out all the time, and you know what children are. A lady came in and bought several things, and asked for a box of Marchpane Magic. There wasn't one left on the stand, so I ran in here to fetch one, and found Tracy'd just pulled one out of the parcel I'd begun opening. I took it from her, and sold it

116

to the lady.'

'I see,' Pollard said. 'Do you by any chance know the name of the lady, Mrs Willis?'

With a feeling of fatalism he watched her shake her head.

'No, I don't,' she said. 'I can't say I paid much heed to her, being so flustered with Tracy in here, and my sister coming to fetch her, and the unpacking not done. But she wasn't a regular—I'm sure of that.'

'Have you any idea what the lady looked like? Was she elderly, for instance, or a young girl?'

'Not really elderly, she wasn't. I'd've noticed that. Not very young, I don't think. But I just can't call her to mind properly.'

'Were there any other customers in the shop while she was here?'

'No, nobody else. I remember running back in here in case Tracy was up to mischief.'

'What about the time when the lady was buying the chocolates?'

Mrs Willis wrinkled her brow, looking like an anxious monkey.

'Round ten o'clock, it must've been, near as no matter.'

Realizing that there was no more to be gained from her, Pollard took the address of the hospital and the sister in Wallington, and rose to go after thanking Mrs Willis, and attempting further reassurance. Toye's first reaction when they were outside on the pavement was gruffly complimentary.

'Hand it to you again, sir, over the Langs this time. No doubt in the world they're in the clear, just as you felt all along.'

'Yes,' Pollard replied, 'they're in the clear all right, as their plane wasn't in till after one. Is there anything further back than Square One, do you know, because that's where we seem to be? Look here, there are things to check on Mrs Willis's statement. The time she picked up the kid, for instance, and the hospital times. You'd better push off and cope with all that, while I go back and put in a report. What we do next is anybody's guess.'

After discussing a few points they parted, Pollard taking the car. He drove back to the Yard torn between satisfaction at the vindication of the Langs, and dismay at finding himself without a single convincing lead to work on.

On reaching his room, he sat down at his desk and grimly addressed himself to making a report on the evidence provided

117

by Mrs Willis. He had barely started when his secretary came in.

'Information on Harrison and Wynne, sir,' the latter said, presenting him with a sheet of typescript.

'Thanks,' Pollard said, taking it without enthusiasm, and running his eye over it.

The next moment he experienced the mental equivalent of a mild electric shock.

'Here,' he said, recalling his secretary from the door, 'get me on to Forensic, will you?'

After a brief delay he found himself through to a scientist colleague in the research department.

'Maitland? Good,' he said. 'I'm interested in a light engineering works. Don't they have cyanide around in a place like that?'

'Sure,' replied the scientist. 'They use it in case hardening. To the uninitiated like you, that's the surface hardening of iron and steel by immersion in a cyanide bath.'

'Oh, yeah?' retorted Pollard. 'Is the stuff kept under lock and key, like dangerous drugs in a hospital?'

'Should be, of course, but probably isn't, as a general rule. Is this your doped chocolates case?'

'It is. Well, thanks for the gen. Now that I've got it from the horse's mouth, it'll help to fill out my report.'

Maitland wished him luck and rang off.

Pollard picked up the report again, and sat looking at it.... Harrison and Wynne Ltd, Light Engineering Works. Managing Director: John E. Bayley....

Dropping it, he began to compose a report for his Assistant Commissioner, now recovered from his cold and back at his post. By midday it had been sent in, and shortly afterwards there arrived a summons to the presence.

Still rather catarrhal but restored to normal good humour, the AC looked up with the hint of a grin as Pollard came in.

'Congratulations,' he remarked. 'Each act provides its quota of the unexpected. Exeunt the Langs in the wake of the bigamous Donald Vickers, and now a light engineer waits in the wings for his cue. What's the curtain going up on this time?'

'I couldn't have answered that question when I came away from Honeydew this morning, sir. But now we know that John Bayley has access to cyanide, and there are reasonable grounds for suspecting him of conspiracy to commit arson, I think it's worth plugging away at a possible link with the Vickers murder, improbable though it seems at this stage.'

The AC cleared his throat noisily, and selected a lozenge from a tin on his desk.

'We'll assume for a moment that such a link exists,' he said. 'This would imply (a) that Mrs Vickers found out about the arson conspiracy, and (b) that John Bayley knew that she had, and came to the rather surprising decision that it was worth taking the risk of murdering her to shut her mouth for good and all. I'd like your comments.'

'Re (b), sir,' Pollard replied, 'it's occurred to me within the past hour that we don't know the final autopsy report on the body found in the burnt house at Roccombe. Suppose the dead chap was knocked on the head?'

The AC shot a glance at him.

'My own thought precisely. It would make the murder of Mrs Vickers a necessity, wouldn't it? What about (a)?'

'I find (a) baffling, sir,' Pollard said frankly. 'I think we can rule out her having discovered the conspiracy before the cruise, so she must have learnt about it during the trip. Having met the Bayleys, I simply can't believe that they would have had conversations about it anywhere they could possibly have been overheard, either on board or on shore. They both give the impression of being very much on the spot.'

'I see that you've got Interpol on to James Bayley?'

'Yes, sir. I know I'm not officially on the arson, but I don't think Colonel Brand of Highcastle's likely to object. A full report on the interview with the Bayleys yesterday evening has gone down to them, and I've asked for the findings of the autopsy on the fire victim. We've got the local chaps enquiring into comings and goings from the Bayleys' house at the time of the fire, too. Then more specifically related to my own case, I thought I'd go along and take a look at Harrison and Wynne's, and see if there's anything to be picked up there. And on the assumption that Mrs Vickers not only found out about the arson conspiracy, but also stuck out her neck, I think another go at the Langs is indicated. In their relief at getting off the hook themselves, they might be able to think more coherently about things that happened on the cruise.'

Slowly masticating his lozenge, the AC sat deep in thought.

'That sounds pretty comprehensive,' he said at last. 'I've no further suggestion to offer. Good luck, then, Pollard, and keep me posted.'

On parting from Pollard some hours earlier, Toye proceeded to carry out his allotted programme with his usual thoroughness. His first call was at the hospital to which Mrs Willis's daughter had been taken on the morning of 1 May. He was there for a considerable time, being passed on from one source of information to another with lengthy waits in between. He wondered during these intervals what it was about a hospital which managed to make you feel completely irrelevant if you weren't a patient. By being quietly persistent he finally got all the information he wanted. As he had expected, it confirmed all the statements made by Mrs Willis about her daughter's admission and her own presence in the hospital on 2 May.

On regaining the outer world he paused on the pavement for a few moments to inhale some antiseptic-free air, and then boarded a bus for Victoria. Here he had a quick snack in the refreshment room, and caught a train for Wallington.

It was an overcast grey day, and leaning back in the corner of a scruffy second-class compartment Toye felt unusually depressed. He was simply rounding up obviously unnecessary confirmation of evidence which had just knocked the bottom out of the case. It's been one ruddy door slamming in your face after another, he thought, disgruntled at having been so convinced of the Langs' guilt himself. After a time, however, relief that Pollard had not made the awful bish of a wrongful arrest gained precedence in his mind over other considerations. He was genuinely, if rather inarticulately devoted to Pollard. And after all, they'd been right up against it before. . . .

An enquiry at the station established that Mrs Fuller, the sister of Mrs Willis, lived within ten minutes' walk, and Toye set off on foot. The house turned out to be a spruce little semi-detached in a side road. He pressed the illuminated bell-push, and set off chimes. Quick steps were audible on the stairs, and the door was opened by a larger and more colourful version of Mrs Willis. Mrs Fuller was confident, quite smartly dressed and sported make-up. A tape measure round her neck and some threads sticking to her clothes suggested that she had been engaged in dressmaking. Toye instinctively sensed a talker, and hastened to introduce himself before she could get launched. He explained that he was making routine enquiries in connection with the Redbay poisoning case.

'My, that's a relief!' she exclaimed. 'My heart was in my throat when you said you were police, after the fright we had over to my sister's Shirley being taken bad in the street, and going off in an ambulance. The police always come round to next-of-kin, don't they, if they can't get you on the phone? We'd like to have one, but what with the rentals going up all the time, and what it costs to have it put in, it just isn't on. My sister told me those chocolates came from Honeydew. Real upset she was. Not very nice for her, is it? Won't you come inside? Not that I've anything to tell you. Maybe you could do with a cuppa? I always make one about now. In there on the right, and make yourself at home. The tea won't take a minute.'

The small front sitting-room was bright and comfortable. Toye took one of the armchairs of the three-piece suite in red imitation leather, and looked about him. Mrs Fuller seemed to have done better for herself than her sister had. There was wall-to-wall carpeting, TV, a big jug of spring flowers on the polished table against the wall, and cheerful and prosperous-looking family photographs dotted about.

Heralded by the rattle of crockery Mrs Fuller swept in with a laden tray.

'There we are!' she exclaimed, setting it down. 'Nothing like a cuppa, is there? Anytime, anywhere, I say? How do you like it?'

Toye asked for a good cup, and two lumps. He accepted a square of home-made gingerbread, and adroitly seized the moment when Mrs Fuller sampled her own cuppa to get in a question about her visit to Honeydew on the morning of Wednesday, 2 May.

'Oh, that's what you've come to ask about, is it?' she said. 'I got there just on ten past ten, if that's what you want to know. My sister wanted me to go to her place to fetch the kiddy before she started for work, but I said it wasn't reasonable, expecting me to get a train before half-past seven in the morning, with my hubby's breakfast to get and clear away. It's all because she's scared of that Mrs Morse. Ridiculous, I call it, with reliable people like Kathleen at a premium, and it isn't as though the wages are all that. So I said I'd be along at the shop by a quarter-past ten, and so I was,' Mrs Fuller ended triumphantly.

With only half his mind on her spate of words, Toye was busy with timing calculations. Mrs Willis had said the lady who had bought the box of Marchpane Whatnot had been in the shop 'about ten'. So Mrs Fuller must only just have missed her.

'Hold it a minute,' he said, cutting into an account of the difficulties of getting little Tracy to eat a proper breakfast. 'This is where I want you to do a bit of thinking back. I'm taking you into my confidence, Mrs Fuller,' he added solemnly. 'We're interested in anyone who bought stuff at Honeydew that Wednesday morning. Can you remember if anyone was in the shop when you got there?'

Mrs Fuller's mouth fell slightly open but she quickly recovered.

'No one at all, there wasn't, while I was in there. I was a bit surprised seeing what a well-known place it is. When I went inside my sister was in the stock room, trying to get some of the parcels from the factory unpacked and checked. She was a bit flustered with Tracy under her feet, so I didn't stop longer than it took to get the kiddy's things on, and...'

Suddenly she broke off. Toye looked at her enquiringly.

'Why, it's just come back to me,' she said. 'There wasn't anyone in the shop, like I said, but just as I turned into Market Court I saw a lady come out of Honeydew. She must've bought several things, because Kathleen—my sister, that is—had put it all in one of their posh carriers with those blessed beehives all over. The lady'd got a car parked outside, and she was unlocking it just as I came up. I know it's rude to stare, but I couldn't help myself, seeing I recognized her, you might say.'

'Recognized her?' Toye's voice sounded oddly hoarse to his own ears.

'That's right. She models for the rag trade. For the older younger woman: I'd put her about thirty. You see her photo in rag trade adverts quite often. I worked for a West End dressmaker before I got married, and I still do a bit for people round here. Now that the boys have left home I've turned the little third bedroom into a workroom, so that I needn't keep on clearing up. I always look carefully at the adverts, so as to know what's being worn. I've got one or two of the lady somewhere in these books.'

She hunted through a pile of magazines which were on a chair in the corner.

'It's this one, I'm sure,' she said, hastily turning the pages. 'Yes, here she is. Lovely suit, isn't it? Ought to be at that price. There's another of her in this month's *Eyeful*. Drat the thing, where's it got to? Funny how the one you want's always at the bottom of the whole lot. This is it. Now then, here we are. Take a look. Knows how to carry off a frock, doesn't she? Mind you, it's the training. She——'

'Mrs Fuller,' Toye said, 'are you prepared to swear that the original of these two photographs is the lady you saw coming out of Honeydew that Wednesday morning?'

'I'd swear it in court any day,' Mrs Fuller assured him buoyantly.

A quarter of an hour later Toye left the house with a signed statement from Mrs Fuller. On reaching the station he found that he had half an hour to wait for a train back to London: an intolerable prospect. Uncharacteristically acting on impulse he dived into a telephone kiosk, and after dialling the Yard number and asking for an extension found himself put through to Pollard.

'Toye here, sir,' he said. 'Speaking from Wallington. An identification of the photograph I mentioned to you was volunteered: there was a copy in the house. Another one of the same person was rustled up, too.'

A piercing whistle of gratified surprise made him move the receiver some inches from his ear.

'Talk about a breakthrough,' Pollard said. 'Here's to you, old chap. Get back here as soon as you can. Something else has come through.'

ELEVEN

On returning to the Yard Toye found Sergeant Longman with Pollard, and the atmosphere almost convivial after the tension of the past few days. He was subjected to congratulatory ragging, and ordered to explain what he had been up to. Trying to conceal all trace of gratification he gave a rather bald account of his visits to the hospital and Mrs Fuller, and handed over the latter's statement.

'One of the things I shall never be able to get over,' Pollard remarked, picking up his copy of *Eyeful*, 'is what can spring from absolutely trivial actions on somebody or other's part. Here's Mrs Bayley taking a look at her photograph in this magazine, and then dropping the thing on the settee open at the page. Perhaps she heard something boiling over on the cooker, or the telephone rang. Then we come along, and Toye decides to park his bottom on the settee instead of on a chair, and the photograph catches his eye.... However, we'd better keep our minds on the job. Highcastle have been on the line, Toye. To cut it short, the final autopsy report on the chap in the fire at Roccombe is that his skull wasn't smashed by the roof caving in on him. A beam fell across his chest and smashed it, but stopped anything much landing on his head. The forensic chaps are satisfied that the skull was fractured by blows from a metal rod or bar, and point out that a set of fire-irons including a poker was found in the wreckage. Tests for blood-stains and so forth aren't on, of course, after the fire and the water from the hoses.'

'Real bit of bad luck for the fire-raiser, that dropout being in the house, and coming up to breathe at an awkward moment,' commented Longman.

'Makes sense of the Bayleys doing Mrs Vickers, though,' Toye said, 'if we take it she found out about the arson, seeing they'd got a murder on their hands as well.'

'From the look of things, a motive's been established,' Pollard agreed, 'but there's a long way to go yet. How the hell *did* she find out? Our only chance of getting a line on that is from the Langs, as far as I can see, and I doubt if she'd have said anything to them about it. Then James Bayley's got to be found and brought back. So far there's no trace of him, according to the latest Interpol report. And up to now neither we nor Highcastle have managed to get on to his trail at the time of the fire. So it's anything but all over bar the shouting.'

Slightly sobered, the other two agreed, and Pollard began to outline his plan of action.

'Highcastle want us to go down, Toye,' he went on. 'Exchange of views, and collaboration over tracing the fire-raiser's movements, etc. I said we'd get the last train down tonight, and be available first thing tomorrow morning. They're fixing us up at the Southgate as usual. Meanwhile Longman's co-ordinating enquiries about James Bayley at this end: we haven't a shred of evidence against him so far, remember. With any luck it may be possible to find someone who saw him turn up at the Trafalgar Terrace house after the John Bayleys went off on the cruise, or even pushing off again for Roccombe on 26 April or thereabouts.'

'What about John Bayley's factory, sir?' Toye asked.

'Dates are important here,' Pollard replied. 'Let's see. The John Bayleys weren't expected back from the cruise before 7 May at the earliest. They had given out that they were going to have a week in Venice after they disembarked. If John Bayley got cyanide from the factory, he must have gone along there very soon after flying back to London on Monday, 30 April, because of the time factor. The chocolates were posted on the following Thursday, and doctoring them would take quite half a day, I should think. Did he just clock in as usual on the Tuesday, and pay an unobtrusive visit to wherever the stuff's kept, or did he pay the place a surprise visit out of hours? All this is over to you and the local chaps you've roped in, Longman. Any further suggestions, either of you?'

After some further discussion the meeting broke up, Longman departing for Camden Town, and Toye for a brief visit to his home before meeting Pollard at Paddington for the nine-thirty pm train to Highcastle.

In view of the heaped state of his In basket, Pollard reluctantly abandoned the idea of a quick dash to Wimbledon, and rang Jane.

'I shan't be back tonight,' he told her, 'but it's not Fulminster. We're going down to Highcastle on the nine-thirty from Paddington.'

Jane gave an exclamation of surprise.

'Highcastle?'

'Yeah. They've got a problem, and we've got a problem, and the two look like heading for a merger, you'll be surprised to hear.'

'What about Fulminster?'

'We'll be taking it in on the way back tomorrow. Not for the purpose I mentioned last night, though. That idea's definitely and finally off.'

'Congratulations,' she said. 'Even if you've still got a problem.'

'I sure have, darling,' he told her, 'but I'd much rather have it this way.'

After further conversation of a purely personal character he rang off, and addressed himself to arrears of work relating to other cases.

As Pollard saw it, the conference at Highcastle police headquarters on the following morning had its amusing side. Colonel

Brand, the Chief Constable, enjoyed the opportunity of stressing the amount and quality of the work his men had put in on the Roccombe arson. Dart, on the strength of being the only person present with working experience of both the arson and the Vickers murder case, felt an obvious sense of superiority in his sombre way.

After discussing the findings of the autopsy they passed on to the forensic experts' report on the fire. Brede House, Roccombe, had been listed as a largely seventeenth-century house of architectural interest, and numerous photographs of it were available. Pollard inspected them, and felt sympathy with Olivia Strode's dismay at the disaster. Brede seemed originally to have been a two-roomed house with a cross-passage, an upper storey having been added at a later date. He noted the rectangular projecting stair turret that Olivia had mentioned, and a massive exterior chimney-breast. There was a single-storey porch, and an attractive round-headed doorway.

The little house and its garden of about a fifth of an acre formed a surprising rural enclave in the built-up centre of Roccombe. Access to it was from a narrow lane joining the town's two main streets, which were roughly parallel to each other. Dart produced a large-scale plan, and pointed out the location of the supermarket whose owners had been anxious to acquire the site for the expansion of their present premises. From the point of view of destruction the fire had been an unqualified success. The roof had fallen in, and only blackened walls and gaping window spaces remained. The structure had been a timber frame of oak filled in with bricks. The latter were cracked and split, but the oak beams, hardened by the passage of time to a steel-like consistency, were still in position although badly charred.

The report stated that the fire had been deliberately started in two places. Rags soaked in paraffin had been used as incendiary material, together with a quantity of newspapers and cardboard which were probably lying about in the partly dismantled house. Traces of wax where both the fires started indicated a timing device involving the burning down of candles.

'Interesting,' Pollard commented. 'The fire is thought to have got going about twelve-thirty am, isn't it? The chap could have rigged things up, and pushed off while there were still people about in the street. Much less noticeable than slinking around in the small hours, with the fire gaining ground rapidly.'

'Quite,' Colonel Brand agreed. 'That struck us at once. Dart, you'd better explain the lines you've been working on.'

'Roccombe's a smallish market town,' the latter said. 'It's got about twelve thousand people. But it's quite a busy little place: centre for a big rural area, and it gets a lot of tourists in the summer. They use it as a base, and go touring round in their cars. It's only a dozen miles from the coast. It's not got what you'd call night-life, though, and people don't keep late hours. All the same, there'd be a few around up to eleven, and a bit after, maybe. We've made house-to-house enquiries about parked cars the night of the fire, and questioned the conductor and some of the passengers on the last bus out, but nothing came of it. The railway's not on: the station closes down at half-past eight. But one of my chaps had the bright idea of calling at the Railway Hotel. It doesn't sound much with a name like that, but it's a fair-sized comfortable place, bucked up by the tourist trade. We found that a chap booked in for the night of the fire, Thursday, 26 April. Gave his name and address as J. Brocken-hurst, 17 Alma Road, Huddersfield. I needn't tell you there's no such place.'

Pollard was suitably complimentary.

'The chap came off the London train, as they call it,' Dart went on. 'It's the connection with the London train here, getting to Roccombe at four-ten if it's on time. It brings back kids who come in to school here, and shoppers, as well as anybody from a distance, so for about five to ten minutes the station's quite busy. So nobody actually noticed the chap arrive, but he seems to have walked over to the hotel, and asked for a room for the night, mentioning that he'd come on the train. It's a bit unusual for people not to come by car these days, so it stuck in the receptionist's mind. She's quite a bright kid, so we've had her over in case you'd like to question her. She's here now.'

'I'm sure you've had all she knows,' Pollard replied tactfully, 'but it sometimes helps to hear it at first hand.'

'It seems a damn silly way for the chap to behave at first sight,' Colonel Brand remarked, 'but when you think it over, it's got points. People notice parked cars, and as you said just now, roaming about in the middle of the night's damn chancy.'

'I agree,' Pollard said. 'If you've got to take a whacking great risk, behaving in a perfectly open way's often your best bet.'

'Shall I take Superintendent Pollard along to see the girl, sir?' Dart asked. 'Three of us might be a bit much for her, don't you think?'

Maureen Webb, receptionist of the Railway Hotel, Roccombe, was a fresh-faced sensible young woman in her early twenties. In answer to Pollard's question about her job, she explained that reception didn't keep you all that busy except in the season, so she lent a hand with other things in the hotel. They hadn't been expecting any arrivals that afternoon, so the gentlemen had had to ring for service. He told her he'd come down on business on the train from London, and just wanted a room for the night. Not dinner, as he was meeting his business contact. They weren't anything like full, so she had no difficulty in fixing him up.

Asked by Pollard if she could describe the visitor, she was less sure of her ground. Quite a tall gentleman, she said, wrinkling her brow. Not young, exactly, round thirty-five, perhaps. Very polite and nice, but not the sort to start telling you all about himself or get fresh. He'd worn horn-rimmed spectacles, and had a brief-case and an overnight case with him. Pressed by Pollard for further details, she thought his hair had been an ordinary sort of brown, nothing to notice specially, and hadn't taken in the colour of his eyes. He'd asked for afternoon tea, which was served to him in the residents' lounge, and about six o'clock he'd stopped at the desk on his way out with his brief-case to ask what time the hotel closed for the night. They only had a night porter in the season, so she'd let him have a key on the usual deposit, in case his business kept him after half-past eleven when they locked up. He'd returned it the next morning when he paid his bill, and gone off to get the train back to London. She'd happened to notice him crossing the road and making for the station.

Pollard asked her a few more questions, but it was plain that she had nothing more to tell him. He thanked her for her help, adding that she had made a valuable contribution to the enquiry into the fire at Roccombe.

She reddened with pleasure.

'A real wicked thing to do, setting fire to a place like that,' she said indignantly, 'and poor Barny Mole burnt to death, dead drunk or not. People back at Roccombe are scared stiff thinking we've got a fire-raiser around.'

'I don't think they need worry about that,' Pollard reassured her. 'We're quite sure this is a case on its own.'

When they had returned to Colonel Brand, Dart went on

128

with his story. No one in the hotel had heard the so-called J. Brockenhurst come in that night, but he must have done, as the chambermaid found him asleep in bed when she took in early tea at eight o'clock the next morning. As Maureen Webb had said, he subsequently breakfasted, paid his bill and departed, presumably by the London train at nine twenty-five am.

Pollard picked up the street plan of Roccombe.

'Is there a garden wall shutting off the house from the lane?' he asked.

'Yes, there is,' Dart replied. 'Another thing which helped the chap. The wall's about six feet, and the old lady who lived there had spikes put on the top to stop kids climbing up. The gate's solid wood, with a good lock. The local estate agent's got one key, and no doubt the Bayleys have another. Once you were through the gate and the supermarket was closed, you could do what you liked without being spotted. Some curtains had been left up, too, so there wouldn't have been any risk of the candle light showing.'

'In fact, the only real risk was being seen going in,' Pollard remarked.

'If he went along after leaving the hotel,' Colonel Brand said, 'it wasn't a bad moment to choose. Shops shut at half-past five, and people soon clear off home, or drop into a pub on the way. Not many would be cutting through the lane at that hour. And if anybody saw a respectably dressed man with a brief-case unlocking the gate, he'd think it was something to do with the estate agent. A prospective buyer, perhaps. The house was up for sale. In any case no one has come forward about it.'

After some further discussion Colonel Brand suggested that all useful ground had been covered, and the conference broke up. Pollard was to lunch with him, and after arranging to meet Toye at the railway station he went off with his host.

It was a good lunch, and he found the Chief Constable pleasant company. Afterwards, when they parted, Pollard found that he had an hour to spare before the Fulminster train, and went for a stroll round the old part of the city. He was admiring some eighteenth-century houses in the cathedral close when a car drew up and parked within a few yards of him. The next moment Olivia Strode got out. They looked at each other in surprise, and she came towards him smiling with hand outstretched, a short comfortable figure in a light summer suit, bareheaded and carrying a shopping-basket.

'How unexpected,' she said, as they shook hands.

'Unexpected and nice,' Pollard replied. 'You know, once or twice during the past few days I've wondered if you would be willing to give me a little more help. I suppose you can't spare a few minutes here and now?'

'Willingly. I've only come in for shopping. What about that seat over there?'

From where they sat flowering trees were a mass of delicate colour against the grey stone of the cathedral.

'They seem particularly good this year,' Olivia said, in reply to a comment from Pollard. 'Are you staying in Highcastle?'

'I came down last night for a conference with your Chief Constable and Inspector Dart, and go on to Fulminster this afternoon.'

She gave him a quick look.

'Fulminster? Isn't that where the Langs live?'

'Yes, it is. In point of fact it's to see them that I'm going there. At the risk of being indiscreet I'll tell you that they're completely cleared. The enquiry has shown that they couldn't possibly have been involved in Mrs Vickers' death.'

Olivia's face expressed her relief.

'I'm profoundly thankful to hear that, Mr Pollard. I've thought about those two young people such a lot. I just couldn't believe that they'd done such a terrible thing. I do hope life will be easier for them now. They both struck me as badly needing a little peace and quiet to grow up in.'

'I think that sums it up very well,' Pollard said.

They sat without speaking for a few moments. A flock of pigeons rose into the air, circled round and returned to the grass where an old lady was scattering largesse. For a moment Olivia was back in the Piazza San Marco.

'Mrs Strode,' Pollard said suddenly, breaking in on her thoughts, 'as I said just now, I think you may be able to help me once again if you're really willing to be bothered.'

'Of course I'm willing,' she replied, 'especially after what you've just told me about the Langs. They may be in the clear from the point of view of the police, but people will still go on talking until the case is finally solved, won't they?'

'They will. Well, I've come down here in connection with the arson at Roccombe. You'll understand that I can't say any more, but I'm quite sure you'll draw certain conclusions. You're a writer, aren't you? Would you be prepared to put down everything that you can remember about Mr and Mrs Bayley that strikes you as even faintly relevant? Never mind how trivial it seems.'

'All right,' she said, after a short pause. 'I'll do my best, but I very much doubt if I'll be able to produce anything likely to help you. The sooner you have it, the better, I suppose?'

'Well, yes, but I don't want to ask the impossible.'

'I'll try to get something off to you by the Sunday afternoon post from Affacombe. If I send it by first-class mail you'll certainly get it by the second delivery on Monday—possibly by the first. Will that do?'

'I'll be very grateful indeed,' Pollard told her, glancing at his watch. 'Now I must be making for my train, unfortunately.'

'I suppose you're obliged to live in London, on account of your job? How I should hate it.'

'It's not so bad out at Wimbledon where we are. Our house is in a quiet road, with quite a decent bit of garden.'

'Wimbledon?' Olivia exclaimed, as they walked in the direction of the main street. 'Why, my son and his wife live there. Do you remember meeting them briefly at Poldens, just before they were married? They've got a house in Uplands Rise.'

'Yes, indeed. I remember them both well. Your son's a solicitor, isn't he?'

'Yes, he's a partner in a London firm. They've a small boy of two, and another baby coming very shortly.'

'We're just a beat ahead of them, then. We've twins of seventeen months. Boy and girl.'

'How simply splendid. Next time I come up we must arrange for the families to meet. David and Julian would love it.'

'So should we,' Pollard said, 'so I hope that's a firm undertaking. I turn down here, don't I? Thank you again, Mrs Strode, and quite apart from your help, it's been a pleasure to meet again.'

Remembering that Drusilla worked at the Fulminster Technical College on Fridays, Pollard decided to allow time for the Langs to have their evening meal before calling on them with Toye that evening. It was after seven when they arrived at the house and rang the appropriate bell. After a short interval someone could be heard running downstairs, and the door was flung open by Keith Lang.

It had been a warm day, and he presented an ungainly figure

in his shorts, open-necked shirt and scuffed scandals. The old-fashioned word hobbledehoy sprang to Pollard's mind, but as he formulated it a change seemed to come over the young man's bearing. The alarm he had registered on recognizing his visitors was replaced by a kind of stoical dignity which lent him presence.

'Good evening,' he said a little breathlessly in reply to Pollard's greeting, looking him straight in the face.

'May we have a few minutes with you and Mrs Lang?' Pollard asked.

'You'd better come in.'

Without looking back Keith led the way up a wide carpeted staircase, and then on again up a steeper one with worn linoleum on the treads. As they reached the second floor of the house there were sounds of washing up from a room at the back.

'Come along a minute, Dru, will you?' Keith called in an expressionless voice.

Pollard and Toye followed him into a sitting-room. In the window overlooking the road was a table with a typewriter and piles of typescript at one end, and some science textbooks and essays at the other. The floor was bare boards with a square of carpet in the middle. There were two elderly armchairs, two upright chairs drawn up to the table, well-filled bookcases, a television set and a gas fire. Gay posters partly covered the faded wallpaper, and fragrance from a jar of white lilac on the mantelpiece filled the air.

They all turned as Drusilla appeared in the doorway, small and vivid in a royal blue mini-frock. She stopped dead, and her hand went involuntarily to her mouth.

Keith strode forward, shut the door, and with unexpected formal courtesy ushered her towards one of the armchairs before taking a defensive stance in front of the fireplace.

Pollard took possession of the other armchair and smiled at them.

'You needn't look as if this is the end of the countdown,' he said. 'There are two reasons for this visit of ours. I'll be blunt. The first is to tell you that the enquiry has reached a point at which we know that neither of you could have been responsible for Mrs Vickers' death.'

The Lang's immediate response was to each other, oblivious of the presence of Pollard and Toye. They exchanged a long look, and Keith came forward and perched on the arm of his wife's chair.

'Thanks for telling us,' he said shakily. 'I won't pretend we haven't been a bit het up. It looked a bit obvious, didn't it?'

'Too obvious,' Pollard replied, 'for people as intelligent as yourselves. You must credit the police with some powers of judgement, you know.'

'It's been hell,' Drusilla said unequivocally, but she had herself in hand. She got to her feet with a degree of poise which astonished Pollard after her behaviour at their first meeting. All this has started her on the growing up process all right, he thought, remembering Olivia Strode's remark. 'We haven't any beer, I'm afraid,' she went on, 'but I can make coffee. The real thing, not instant.'

'A cup of coffee would be fine,' Pollard said, 'wouldn't it, Sergeant?'

While Drusilla was in the kitchen he tried to reduce tension by talking to Keith about his writing.

'I suppose some people would call me an escapist,' the young man said in the course of conversation. 'My new novel's been the only thing that's kept me from going round the bend since all this business blew up. Drusilla's felt the same about her job.'

'And why not?' Pollard asked. 'Surely literature and science are as real as the ups and downs of day-to-day living?'

Keith grinned, his rather heavy face lighting up attractively.

'You're making me revise my image of a copper,' he said. 'Up to now it seems to have been oversimplified. I want to say that you've treated us jolly decently, and we're grateful. Anything we can do—you know. Here's the coffee.'

The coffee was excellent, and Pollard praised it.

'Sergeant Toye and I have got to get back to London tonight,' he said, 'so I'd better get on with the second reason for this visit. Do you remember my ringing you at Redbay vicarage?'

They nodded, looking puzzled.

'About that water-colour, you mean?' Drusilla asked.

'About the artist who'd painted it. All I can say at the moment is that we're still interested in the subject. You told me, Mrs Lang, that Mrs Vickers had raised it with a Mr John Bayley during the cruise. During one of the shore excursions, I think you said. Will you both try to remember all you can about the conversation between them on this occasion?'

Silence descended. Drusilla leant forward, resting her elbows on her knees, her chin cupped in her hands. Keith stared out of the window, frowning in his concentration. Toye took out his notebook.

Keith was the first to speak.

'It was when we were on Delos,' he said, 'waiting in the Slave Market. The harbour's awfully shallow, and everyone had to be brought ashore in small boats. It took quite a long time, and people were sitting around waiting for the last boat-loads, so that the talk we were going to have could start.'

'Yes,' Drusilla took up, 'there was quite a crowd there by the time we came along. It's no good wrapping things up, so I'll say right away that one of the worst things about being with Aunt Audrey was the way she tried to cotton on to people. It made you hot under the collar. As soon as we got to the Slave Market she spotted the Bayleys, and made a beeline for them. We tagged along after her, trying to look as though we didn't belong.'

'Had Mrs Vickers already mentioned the picture to you?' Pollard asked.

'Oh, Lord, yes,' Keith replied. 'For some reason she suddenly thought about it the night before, and had kept on and on about it until we were browned off.'

'Aunt Audrey started off with the Bayleys with her interest-in-art line,' Drusilla continued. 'Then she said she'd one of Mr Bayley's pictures, and how delighted she was to meet him. They both stared at her, and he said she was quite mistaken, and he'd never painted anything in his life. She just wouldn't believe him, and went all arch and girlish, although anyone could see they were getting really annoyed. In the end he bit her head off, but she crowed triumphantly, and said she'd got his address in London, and would be turning up to see his studio, and perhaps buy another picture.'

'What did Mr Bayley say to that?' Pollard asked.

'He didn't,' Keith contributed. 'He was puce with rage by this time, and his wife cut in before he hit the roof. She took the freezing line, and said she didn't receive uninvited guests. Then they got up and walked off. I saw them make meaning faces at Mrs Strode, and she reciprocated.'

'It was things like this which simply got us on the raw,' Drusilla said. 'Oh, yes, I know Aunt Audrey was a psychological mess, and probably couldn't help it, but honestly, it was the end.'

'I can understand how you felt,' Pollard remarked, his mind

more than half occupied with the Bayleys' determination to prevent a visit from Audrey Vickers. Was it quite understandable, or could it have a deeper significance? It was difficult to see what this could be. How might a call at the Trafalgar Terrace house help her to discover about the arson?

'Have we been any help?' he heard Keith ask.

'You've given me something to worry at,' he replied.

'I suppose nothing can be done about Aunt Audrey's affairs until it's found out who sent her the chocolates?' Drusilla said suddenly. 'After Mr Partridge said she'd told him to make her a new will cutting me right out I felt I didn't want her money, but he says he's sure she didn't really mean to sign it in the end, but was just blowing her top. So Keith and I think it's all right. We shall give a lot to her favourite charities, anyway.'

Pollard mentally awarded an accolade to Mr Partridge for adroitness.

'Of course we shan't go all lush or anything,' Keith said seriously. 'I shall go on writing, and Drusilla's going to get a research job. We think we'd like to go back to Oxford. We'll have decent holidays, though. Not the Costa Brava sort, naturally.'

'Holidays on our own,' Drusilla said dreamily. 'You know, I shall always think Aunt Audrey must have had a brainstorm or something on the Acropolis that morning. It was after that that things really went wrong.'

'Well,' Pollard said, 'Sergeant Toye and I must make for the station. Is there any means of ringing for a taxi?'

'Good Lord, we'll run you down,' Keith said, leaping to his feet. 'The Mini's on the way out, but she's all right for short distances.'

Pollard thanked him, avoiding Toye's eye as he did so.

They crammed into the battered little car, Pollard in front because of his long legs, and Toye and Drusilla behind. Keith drove on his brakes, and Pollard had rewarding glimpses of Toye's expression in the driving mirror.

On their arrival they stood chatting for a few moments outside the station entrance before saying goodbye. After they had parted Pollard glanced back to see the pair making for the Mini, absorbed in each other and in conversation.

'Look at 'em,' he said. 'How beautiful upon the mountains are the feet of him that bringeth good tidings.'

'That's right,' agreed Toye, who had belonged to a choral society in his more leisured youth.

TWELVE

Saturday morning brought no news of the whereabouts of James Bayley. Pollard thankfully seized the opportunity of re-appraising the rapid developments of the past few days. In spite of the progress made he felt very far from confident of the outcome, and had to curb his irritation at what he felt to be unwarranted optimism on the part of Toye and Longman.

'Now then,' he said, 'before we get on to what you've dug up in Camden Town, Longman, I want to try to sum up what's come out of these trips to Highcastle and Fulminster. Not much in my opinion. Isolated bits of information may be valuable in themselves, but unless you can fit them into the pattern of the case as a whole they're not much help at this stage. Take Highcastle first. It's useful that the hotel reception-ist at Roccombe could almost certainly identify James Bayley, but the chap's got to be found and brought back here first. All his comings and goings down there, and the fire-raising dodges he used are primarily the arson case's pigeon, not ours. On to Fulminster, then. At first sight what we got from the Langs looks pretty good, and I admit that they're convincing as wit-nesses. But all that's really happened is that we've exchanged one problem for another. Up to now we've been worrying away at how Audrey Vickers managed to find out about the arson conspiracy. Now it looks as though she hadn't found out at the time of the conversation with the Bayleys about the water-colour, but that she was bound to if she carried out her threat of visiting them at Trafalgar Terrace. She seems to have signed her own death warrant by letting on that she'd got the address. What the hell does one make of that?'

There was a lengthy silence. Finally Toye muttered some-thing about blackmail.

'If you mean saying she'd call was a threat to blackmail them, it implies that she'd already got on to the arson,' Pollard re-plied, 'which I'm now inclined to doubt. Besides, would she set about blackmail in that flamboyant sort of way, more or less announcing her intentions in a public gathering? I suppose she might. The woman was an extrovert, and her mental balance on a knife-edge from all accounts. However, all this had better go into cold storage for the moment. Let's hear what you've managed to unearth, Longman, while Toye and I have been on the road.'

Detective-Sergeant Longman, a Londoner born and bred, had a flair for nosing out information about such of his fellow-citizens as the police were interested in. With the help of the men of the district station he had covered a good deal of ground during the past day and a half.

The Bayleys did not appear to be in financial difficulties, but clearly lived it up and got through a good bit of money. They had spent a packet in modernizing and doing up the house, and moved in a well-to-do circle of friends. Harrison and Wynne were doing well, and there were rumours of plans to extend operations. John Bayley had an interest in the firm as well as being its managing director, and it would obviously be an opportune moment for him to put some more money into it. As an employer he was considered fair without being liked. A man had described him to Longman over a drink in a pub as a bloke who did the right thing by you because it paid in the long run. Mrs Bayley was thought to pull down quite a packet through her modelling. Longman had been unable to pick up anything about James Bayley beyond the fact of his existence and occasional appearances at the house.

'I had my first break over him, sir,' Longman went on. 'There's one house in Trafalgar Terrace being converted now, with workmen still in. It's Number Twenty, quite near the Bayleys' place. I dressed down for the part, and went lounging along and got chatting with an old codger whose job seemed to be propping up ladders. No having much to occupy his mind, he'd got to know the comings and goings of the people round about, so I worked him round to the Bayleys. That led him on nicely to where the money was, and he volunteered the statement that he'd seen them going off for a holiday about a month back, piling the luggage into their swell car. I said something about break-ins, and it being risky leaving your house with no-body in it these days, and he said they must've got a friend to live there part of the time, as he'd seen a chap coming in and brakes all round ... petrol fumes ... Go ... roar of engines this, and tried the old boy out by suggesting the husband had come back first, but he was quite ratty, saying his chap was different, and wore hornrims. He said he dressed casual, not the city gent, like the bloke the house belonged to.'

'A bit indefinite, but it might come in useful. Did you manage

137

to get anything in the way of dates?' Pollard asked.

'The old boy said that this chap must have gone off a day or two before the owners came home, as he didn't see him around any more. I didn't like to seem too interested.'

'Quite right. What about the factory set-up?'

Longman said that one of the constables from the local station had given him some useful information here, as his beat covered the factory although he'd never been inside the place. Harrison and Wynne had a night-watchman, two, in fact, both pensioners. One was on duty on Saturday to Tuesday nights inclusive, and the other did the remaining three nights of the week. They changed over every fourth week.

'The constable found out for me that Horace Bidlake, who was on for the nights of 30 April and 1 May, will be there this weekend, if you should feel like going along, sir,' Longman concluded.

'If John Bayley collected some cyanide during normal working hours,' Pollard said reflectively, 'I don't think we'll ever be able to prove it. He'd know the safe moment to choose. But if we could find out that he'd been along to the factory when the place was closed down for the night, that's a possible bit of circumstantial evidence. What yarn could we pitch to the night-watchman?'

This matter was discussed at some length, Toye insisting that enquiries into motor accidents had worn thin by now. Longman suggested a police enquiry into a new break-in dodge: chaps with faked credentials from the gas board, for instance, saying there was trouble in the next street, and there must be an airlock or something on Harrison and Wynne's premises.

'That sounds OK,' Pollard said. 'What time had we better make it?'

This being settled, he commended Longman for having done a good job, and sent him off with Toye for an afternoon's break.

He had intended to take one himself, but after they had gone he did not leave immediately. He sat on at his desk, once again reviewing the events of the past week, each one a stage in the evolution of a case which had looked so straightforward at first, and subsequently shown a propensity to the most unforeseen developments. Now it had really boiled down to two basic questions: where was James Bayley, and why did Audrey Vickers' threat to call on the Bayleys make her so potentially dangerous to them that they decided to murder her?

It's up to Interpol to get James traced, Pollard thought, but the second problem's mine, and I'm stuck, let's face it. . . .

An unnerving idea flashed into his mind, an echo from a far-off science lesson in his schooldays. . . . If you ask the wrong question, the master had said, don't expect to get the right answer. . . . Was it possible that somehow he, Pollard, was asking the wrong question about Audrey Vickers getting on to the arson which had ended so disastrously in the dropout's murder?

Suddenly conscious of the mental blank of tiredness, he got abruptly to his feet as the first stage of going home.

Jane had kept his lunch hot in the oven, and while the twins had their afternoon sleep he sat with her in the garden, talking a little at first, and then dropping off to sleep over the newspaper. Later he woke much refreshed, and mowed the lawn, watched by Andrew and Rose from the security of a playpen. When the mowing was finished they were released, and Rose walked unsupported, if unsteadily, from one parent to another. This achievement was studiously ignored by her brother, who employed himself in crawling at lightning speed towards the rubbish heap, from which Pollard kept patiently retrieving him.

'I'd better get tea,' Jane said after a time. 'If we put him back in the playpen he'll only roar and shake the bars, and old Mrs Lee next door will look pointedly over the wall. Bringing up children positively bristles with difficulties, doesn't it? So does keeping a CID husband adequately fed, incidentally. If you're leaving for the Yard at eight, we'd better have a meal of sorts at half-past seven.'

'Mr Bidlake?' Pollard asked the elderly unshaven face peering at him through the grille in Messrs Harrison and Wynne's locked gates. 'We're CID officers. I can't pass you my card through that contraption, but you can ring the local station before you open up, if you like. I'm Detective-Superintendent Pollard of New Scotland Yard.'

Mr Bidlake was sharp-featured, with a knowing eye which he brought to bear on Pollard. The result of the inspection was apparently satisfactory, as he proceeded to unlock the wicket and let the three Yard men in.

' 'Orace Bidlake's the name,' he said, holding the proffered card at a distance and purporting to read it. 'Wot's the big idea, guv? Brought along 'alf the blinkin' Yard, aincher?'

139

'The wide boys are trying out a new dodge in North London,' Pollard told him. 'Knock up a night-watchman like yourself, hand in a fake card from the electricity board or the water board, and say the trouble in the next street has been traced to the factory, and can they take a look? You let 'em in, and while you're all going to take a look, you never know what hit you. Next morning a lorry goes out all bright and early and loaded up. Get the idea?'

'There ain't bin none o' that rahnd 'ere,' Mr Bidlake told him. 'Two years, we've 'ad, without a break-in.'

'You've been lucky. It's a big place for one man to cover,' Pollard remarked, looking about him.

The Gambit worked instantly. Horace Bidlake carefully re-locked and bolted the wicket gate, and led off the part on an escorted tour of the premises, giving a running commentary on the area he was expected to cover, and the conscientiousness with which he carried out his rounds.

As far as Pollard could see, the factory buildings were a hollow square, the central space including a loading bay for lorries. It looked as though anyone with the necessary keys could pass freely from one section to another, under cover all the time.

By prearrangement with Toye and Longman conversation was kept going briskly. Towards the end of the tour Pollard asked casually if night shifts were worked.

'I should think you'd be glad of a bit of company,' he said. 'It must be a dreary business with no one to speak to all night.'

No, they'd never worked night shifts in his time, the old man told him, although he'd heard they did in the war, when they were on Government contracts. It was a lonely sort of job, all right, but you got used to it, like everything else. It wasn't above three or four times a year you were knocked up, usually by one of the staff who'd left something behind. Not that he minded if they did: it was a break, and a chance to pass the time of night.

'Glad we've been along to buck you up tonight,' Pollard said. 'How long is it since anybody else did, I wonder?'

'Matterer las' Monday week, as it 'appens,' Horace Bidlake told him. 'I reckins I've 'ad me quoter fer the nex' 'arf-year. Boss came in, rahnd eleven, 'twas. Said 'e'd bin called back urgent from 'is 'oliday, an' wanted some pipers from 'is desk in 'is orfice.'

At this point they had arrived back at the small room near the gates which the nightwatchman used as a base. It was provided with an electric kettle, and this was flanked by a bottle of milk and a collection of tins.

'Did you offer the boss a cuppa, Dad?' Longman enquired.

Horace Bidlake cackled.

' 'Is Nibs? Not bloody likely. Too 'igh an' mighty, 'im. Anyways, I was at the dratted telephone mos' o' the time 'e was in.'

'Your missis, I bet,' Longman remarked. 'Wanting to find out if you'd brought along a nice young bird with you.'

This pleasantry evoked an even louder cackle. No, it wasn't the missis, the old man replied, seeing that he'd buried her three years back. Some ruddy foreign chap about an order. He'd had to write down no end of stuff, which didn't come easy, seeing he'd left school at fourteen, before the Kaiser's war. Then after all it turned out they'd rung the wrong number. He'd told the chap what he thought. Why, even the boss standing there waiting to be locked up after had a good laugh for once.

Suitable comments were made, and Pollard offered advice on dealing with callers armed with bogus credentials and probably guns as well before the Yard party withdrew in good order.

'All circumstantial,' Pollard said when they got outside, 'but it could be damn useful to the prosecution if the case ever gets to court. Nice touch about the phone call being made by a foreigner.'

'Good way of disguising your voice,' Toye agreed, 'Mrs Bayley's got a deepish one, when you come to think of it.'

As they drove home Pollard roused himself to congratulate Longman once again.

'You've done a first-rate job round here,' he said.

The evening was close, and he found the traffic jams of Saturday night almost unbearable.... Stop ... screech of brakes all round ... petrol fumes.... Go ... roar of engines and horn blasts from the frenziedly impatient...

Dismissing the thought of wrong questions from his mind, he fell to speculating about the ultimate outcome of the unrestricted growth of motor traffic in a small over-populated island.

Two hundred miles away the village of Affacombe was experiencing its own Saturday night traffic problem, and Olivia Strode was thinking along lines very similar to Detective-Superintendent Pollard in North London. The village was an exceptionally attractive one, and its pub, the Priory Arms, known for its friendliness and beer. With the increase of car ownership in the neighbourhood it was drawing patrons from an ever-widening area, especially on Saturday evenings, when the narrow village street became choked with cars, and echoed to the noise of manoeuvring in low gear and slamming doors. The natives complained bitterly about being kept out of their own pub and the disruption of their peace and quiet, while Ted Cummings, the landlord, asked if he was expected to turn away good money for other people's convenience.

As Olivia Strode came out of her cottage two leather-clad figures tore up the street on screaming scooters, and a few moments later she had to squeeze between two parked cars to allow another to pass. It was a relief to turn in at the gate of Crossways, the home of her daughter-in-law's parents.

In her handbag she was carrying a collection of little yellow boxes containing the first consignment of the colour slides from Charles Moreton-Blake's photographs taken during the cruise. She did not possess a projector herself, and had been invited to view the slides on Colonel Winship's.

Charles Moreton-Blake was an enthusiast, and had recorded the holiday fully from the moment of arrival at Heathrow on the day of departure. There were excellent shots of the journey from the airport into Venice by the motor launch, especially those taken along the Grand Canal. To Olivia they brought back the sheer delight of this early stage of her holiday, and to her relief she saw that the Winships were enjoying them almost as much as she was.

'That must be the last of the Grand Canal,' she said. 'Here's the San Marco boat station where we went ashore. The next lot must be San Marco itself, and the Piazza.'

This set, she thought, was even better than the last. Charles had taken the splendid façade of the basilica from many angles, and in the course of the afternoon had found most attractive subjects in the Piazza among the holiday crowds and the ubiquitous pigeons. A tiny dark-eyed child waved from the back of a porphyry lion. A balloon seller with his load of brilliant colour grinned with a delighted flash of white teeth. An old man dozed on the edge at the foot of the campanile, a pigeon perching on the toe of his boot.

At the tables in the front row of Florian's people were...

Olivia fell silent as she stared, suddenly alerted.

'OK for the next?'

Hugh Winship's voice roused her.

'So sorry,' she said. 'I recognized those two people on the right. They were at our table on the cruise.'

'The couple where the man's writing something on a newspaper?' Barbara Winship asked. 'No, he's drawing, isn't he? I like the woman's hair-do.'

'That's the couple,' Olivia replied absently. 'Yes, he's drawing, very competently. They left the paper behind.'

At ten minutes past eleven Pollard drove thankfully into his garage, having noticed with pleasure that there was a light in the sitting-room. Jane was still up.

A few moments later, as he put his latchkey in to the lock, he was astonished to hear a male voice through the curtained but open window. He let himself in, speculating with exasperation about the visitor's identity. As he opened the door of the sitting-room a vaguely familiar youngish man got up.

'Darling, this is David Strode,' Jane said. 'You've met before, I gather?'

'Of course!' Pollard exclaimed. 'I remember you perfectly well now. It was only yesterday that I ran into your mother in Highcastle, and she told me that you and your wife live quite near.'

'We're in Uplands Rise,' David Strode said. 'I do apologize for turning up at this hour, but my mother's been on the line with a message for you which she says may be very important. She thought your number probably wasn't in the book, and the simplest thing was to get on to you through me.'

Jane Pollard murmured something about the children, and slipped away.

'Do sit down,' Pollard said. 'I see Jane's produced some beer. Join me in another, won't you?'

'Thanks, I will ... Well, here's to your case, which I gather is a snorter. Cheers.'

'Cheers,' Pollard replied, raising his glass.

'Now, about this message,' David Strode went on. 'I must say it sounds a bit cryptic to me, but my mamma has a clear way of putting things, and I think I've got it right. You're interested in a certain couple who were on the cruise, I take it? She didn't name them, of course.'

Pollard assented.

'Well, it appears that she saw them for the first time in Venice, where the party had an afternoon for sightseeing before they embarked. She was with friends, the Moreton-Blakes, and they were heading for one of the open-air cafés in St Mark's Square. Just as they arrived this couple got up from a table in the sun and walked away, and my mother and the Moreton-Blakes took it over. They—the couple, that is—had left quite a bit of debris behind, including a copy of the day's *Express*. The space at the top above the headlines was covered with clever little sketches of tourists and pigeons and what-have-you. I say, is this making any sense?'

With barely credible illumination flooding into his mind, Pollard nodded without speaking. David Strode glanced at him and went on.

'Charles Moreton-Blake's keen on photography, and among other things he took various shots of the holiday crowds during the afternoon. He sent the colour slides down for my mother to see, and they arrived this morning. This evening my father-in-law put them through his projector for her. One of them turned out to be this couple sitting at the café table, and the man was sketching on the *Express*. She thought it might be relevant, as she suddenly remembered your asking if she'd seen either of the couple painting.'

There followed a pregnant silence.

'My God,' said Pollard slowly, 'so that was why they couldn't risk Audrey Vickers turning up at the house and running into John Bayley. She——'

The telephone rang clamorously. He swore briefly and got up.

'Excuse me, will you?' he said, going out of the room.

Still slightly bemused by the revelation he had just received, the news that James Bayley had been located at Sirmione came as an anticlimax. The message, telephoned through from the Yard, went on to say that the Englishman had taken a room in the town, and appeared to be spending his time in painting. He was being kept under observation pending instructions.

'OK,' Pollard said. 'Thanks.'

He stood in the hall for a few moments, mechanically registering the fact that Jane was running a bath. Then he returned to David Strode, who looked up with interest.

'I take it this is a matter of identification?' the latter said.

'Yes,' Pollard replied, 'but I can see that it'll have to be absolutely conclusive to satisfy you legal chaps. Do you know, I think we may be asking Mrs Strode to fly out to Italy on Monday?'

THIRTEEN

On Sunday morning a series of telephone calls resulted in a meeting between Pollard and his Assistant Commissioner at the Yard. The latter, back-tilted in his chair and contemplating the ceiling, listened to the account of the latest developments in the case without interruption.

'Interest in this absorbing drama continues to be well maintained,' he remarked when Pollard came to an end. 'Let us assume for a moment that Mrs Strode agrees to fly out to Italy and identify James Bayley as the man she knew on the cruise as John Bayley, how are you going to handle the encounter?'

'My idea is to confront him with her, sir, so that he can't dispute the identification convincingly. I think it should be possible to take him off his guard. Then, when he hears that a murder was committed in connection with the arson, I'm convinced he'll come back voluntarily. Of course he'll realize that he faces a charge of conspiracy to commit arson, but consider his sister's position. Her husband is going to be charged with murder, and she herself as an accessory, in addition to the arson charge.'

The Assistant Commissioner thought this over.

'Why are you so sure that James doesn't know about the Roccombe murder, Pollard? All three Bayleys may have been in contact in Venice on 28 April, when James and John resumed their real identities.'

'In my opinion, sir,' Pollard replied, 'John's attitude to James is a key factor in the whole affair. It would have been so much simpler for James to fire the house while John and his wife were on the cruise. Because of James's unpredictable comings and goings he'd have had a very good chance of clearing the country before Highcastle got on to his trail—if they ever did. And this way, the complicated and risky identity swop wouldn't have been necessary. The fact that John Bayley decided that he must do the job himself shows that he and his wife felt that James would make a mess of it. When I saw them at Trafalgar Terrace, it stood out a mile that John had no use for James, and that while Mrs Bayley was obviously very fond of her brother, she had no illusions about his vagueness and casualness. Because of this, I can't believe that John would tell James about the Roccombe murder, even if they all three met in Venice at the end of the cruise, which I think is unlikely. It would have been very dicey with all the *Penelope* crowd milling around sightseeing. A murder isn't the sort of thing you'd confide to a chap you considered unreliable. But as far as the impersonation went, James sounds the type who'd consider it a good joke, and no doubt he was going to get his whack from the insurance and the ultimate sale of the site to the supermarket people.'

'I think all that's an interpretation which could pass muster,' the AC remarked cautiously after a further pause.

'Reverting to John Bayley's opinion of James, sir,' Pollard said, 'I want to make it clear that Sergeant Toye should have the credit for getting on to this almost at the start. After we'd interviewed the John Bayleys he remarked that you wouldn't expect an artist chap to be what you'd call dependable on a job like arson.'

The AC nodded.

'He spotted that photograph of Mrs Bayley, too, didn't he? Always a sound chap, Toye, and working with you, Pollard, seems to have put a spark into him. We'll bear him in mind. Now, then, let's accept for purposes of argument that James Bayley rallies to his sister's support and comes straight home, where do you propose to go from there?'

'I suggest confronting all three Bayleys with each other, sir, and in the resulting tension over the Roccombe murder, charge the John Bayleys with the murder of Audrey Vickers. I feel pretty confident that this further shock will produce some useful admissions.'

'And you feel justified in asking the taxpayers to foot the bill for this jaunt to Italy?' the AC enquired with an apparent irrelevance which Pollard rightly interpreted as acceptance of his plan.

'Well, yes, sir. I doubt if it'll cost more in the end than letting the enquiry run on.'

'All right, then, you can go ahead, Pollard. But if the whole thing misfires, on your head be it, remember. We'll expect you to contact us from Italy about getting things lined up at this end.'

Olivia Strode found that she had boarded a plane for Milan and become airborne almost without realizing it. Once again she had a window seat, but this time a thick layer of cotton wool clouds cut off all view of the earth beneath and increased the sense of isolation. She turned to Pollard, who caught her eye and smiled back.

'Not feeling too unhappy about it all, are you, Mrs Strode?' he asked.

'It's like being in a worrying sort of dream which began when you rang me at lunch-time yesterday,' she told him. 'I've been trying to clear my mind. Right down inside me I know I'm glad to be helping to get the whole horrible business sorted out. It's the cold-blooded precautionary killing of Audrey Vickers that I find so intolerable, worse than the murder of the poor old drunk at Roccombe, because that obviously wasn't planned. Hideously ruthless, of course, but somehow not quite so repulsive.'

'Ruthlessness has a nasty habit of increasing by geometrical progression,' Pollard said. 'Look at the Nazis, for instance. I wish you hadn't to go through this sort of experience for a second time in your life, although a bit of me is quite glad for a layman to know what hunting down another human being feels like, whatever crime's involved. . . . I'd like you to tell me some more about James Bayley, if you will.'

'I liked him,' Olivia said slowly, 'while right from the first I rather took agin Mrs Bayley. I felt there was something so hard about her—hard as nails was the phrase I used to myself. I remember wondering how they had come to marry. He's a relaxed, good-humoured sort of man, essentially carefree. I'm quite sure he could be tiresomely inconsiderate in everyday life, but it would be from sheer thoughtlessness. Mrs Bayley was always polite to people, but now that I look back, I can see that there was a lot of underlying tension about her. Of course, she must have been on pins the whole time in case James lost grip, and said or did something which might give the show away. One realized that she was very much the dominant partner. But one thing I'm certain about is that she was sincerely fond of him, and he was of her, though to a lesser degree. The relationship between brother and sister can mean a lot, can't it?'

Pollard agreed.

'It's certainly a strong emotional link between our assorted twins,' he said, diverting the conversation into more enjoyable channels.

Dinner was served on board the aircraft, and the flight seemed to pass quickly. It was late when they landed at Milan, however, and Olivia was glad to get to their hotel in view of a very early start for Sirmione the next morning. She was tired, and fell asleep almost as soon as she got into bed after a pleasantly relaxing hot bath.

She was awakened by a waiter with rolls and coffee, and looked at her watch in alarm, but there was plenty of time to breakfast, dress and meet Pollard in the hotel lounge. He was already waiting for her as she stepped out of the lift, and the sight of him was reassuring, She would have been astonished to learn that reassurance was mutual: her composure quietened any remaining qualms he was feeling about the day's programme.

'At any rate you can get a fleeting glimpse of one of the wonders of Milan,' he said in the taxi. 'Look at that!'

Olivia gasped at a soaring skyscraper, ethereal in its slenderness.

'I wish I could have taken you to the cathedral,' he told her, 'but if James Bayley's painting, he'll be out in the morning light, and easy to track down. He may pack it in later, and go off somewhere.'

'Not to worry,' she replied. 'I'd rather get it over. I don't think I could sightsee very intelligently at the moment.'

Later, when the train had at last cleared the industrial sprawl of the city, she was fascinated to see at ground level the ancient ordered landscape which she had gazed down on during the flights to and from Venice. Here it all was: the endless, endless plain, the silver lines of irrigation canals, and the rows of poplars. Files of women were at work with their hoes in the assiduously cultivated fields. Clusters of farm buildings with an air of immemorial antiquity flashed past as the train roared ahead. Once again the sky was cloudless, and far away to the north she thought she could detect the Alps in the blue mistiness of the horizon.

After a time she felt anxious about the part she was to play at Sirmione, and began to question Pollard.

'I'm sure you must think it's extraordinary to me not to have the whole thing sewn up,' he said, 'but I feel it's going to be wiser to play it by ear. You know the chap at first hand, and I don't. Much the easiest thing will be if he recognizes you spontaneously. Let's hope for that, and if it doesn't come off, then I'll weigh in. We're getting along, and ought to be at Desenzano in about twenty minutes now.'

On arrival they were given an enthusiastic welcome by a senior member of the local Questura. When congratulated on his command of English, he assured them that his regiment had been the first, the very first to go over to the Allies in 1944, and he had many good English friends. . . . He had visited England, too, several times. . . .

Olivia was ceremoniously ushered into the back of a waiting car, and they drove off at breathtaking speed. Pollard, in the passenger seat in front, was soon being given a voluble account of the tracing of James Bayley, in the course of which his informant frequently removed both hands from the steering-wheel in expressive gesture. They must drive on quite a different principle here, she thought, as the car overtook another with reckless abandon and furious horn blasts, missing an oncoming vehicle by inches.

Snatches of the monologue in front floated back to her. James Bayley, she gathered, was out painting, at somewhere called La Grotta di Catullo. This sounded like a cave, and she felt puzzled. By this time, however, they had ceached the outskirts of Sirmione. She received a series of rapid impressions: a castle with crenellated towers, cascades of roses, glimpses of the azure blue of Lake Garda, bronzed holidaymakers, hotels, cafés, more and more roses. Beyond the little town they overtook fantasy, a little brightly painted train with open carriages and striped awnings, incredibly running along the road. Then the car shot to a standstill outside the gates, not of a cavern but of an ancient olive grove, grey-green, silver and gnarled in the sunlight.

'La Grotta di Catullo,' their escort announced with sweeping gesture and evident pride. 'Ver' fine. All tourists come 'ere. First we take a coffee, yes?'

At this point a younger man in uniform emerged from a small café just inside the entrance. There was a rapid exchange in Italian, and Pollard learnt that the Englishman was painting over there . . . a little distance only, by the antiquities.

He thanked them, and contrived to by-pass the taking of a coffee without giving offence.

'Shall we go along, then?' he said to Olivia.

She had been waiting in the background with the feeling of unreality that the imminence of a strongly anticipated moment brings. The place itself enhanced the feeling: the incredible blueness of sky and sea, the blazing pools of poppies under the olive trees, the broken colonnade witnessing to some long-forgotten aspiration. It was a stage-setting for a small human drama in which she must play her part.

A man was painting, wholly absorbed. His fair hair looked bleached against his bronzed skin. His clothes were comfortably dilapidated, and painting gear littered the grass beside him.

As Olivia approached with Pollard she instinctively stopped, and waited. In the act of throwing down a brush and selecting another the artist caught sight of her, stared, surfaced and grinned broadly.

'Good Lord, it's Mrs Strode!' he exclaimed. 'I'd no idea you were staying on in Italy.'

She found herself unable to speak and looking at him compassionately. He reacted with a puzzled expression, which after a quick glance at Pollard, became one of wariness.

'Mrs Strode,' came Pollard's voice, 'this gentleman appears to know you. Do you know him?'

'We were recently passengers on the same cruise,' she heard herself saying. 'I knew him as Mr John Bayley.'

'He is, in fact, Mr James Bayley,' Pollard went on, 'and is wanted in connection with a conspiracy to commit arson. Thank you, Mrs Strode.'

At Pollard's slight dismissive nod she turned and walked away under the trees.

The two men remained, eyeing each other steadily. Suddenly James Bayley flung back his head and laughed.

'My God, it's funny,' he said. 'With the world in the bloody mess it is, a British bobby comes tailing half across Europe about a semi-derelict house being fired.'

'If it was merely a question of arson,' Pollard told him, 'I shouldn't be here.'

The other stared at him blankly.

'I'm not with you.'

'A man's body was found in the ruins of the house.'

James Bayley continued to stare, but now with an appalled expression.

'My God,' he said again, 'how bloody awful. He must have been asleep, or something.'

'The man didn't die as a result of the fire,' Pollard replied, watching narrowly. 'It has been established by forensic experts that his skull was fractured by a series of blows from a metal object.'

There was a tense silence.

'So what?' James Bayley demanded loudly and violently.

'Your brother-in-law, Mr John Bayley, your sister and you yourself, face a charge of conspiracy in connection with the arson. In addition, Mr John Bayley faces a murder charge, and his wife one of being an accessory to the crime.'

With an abrupt movement James Bayley began to sweep his belongings into a painting satchel.

'I'm returning with you,' he said curtly.

Precisely at nine-thirty pm that evening the John Bayleys were shown into Pollard's room at the Yard. As he rose to greet them they were tautly polite.

'Well, we've come along here as you asked, Superintendent, and at some inconvenience, I may tell you,' John Bayley said. 'However, I suppose it's preferable to trekking down to Roccombe again.'

'I'm sick to death of the whole business,' Lorna Bayley added. 'Why on earth was I ever landed with the blasted place? I should have refused the bequest. It's been a perfect curse from first to last.'

Pollard invited them both to sit down. Chairs were drawn forward by Sergeant Longman and accepted with marked ill grace.

'We now have information which makes it possible to clear up the whole business of the fire at Mrs Bayley's house,' Pollard said in an official tone, 'and it's for this purpose that you have been asked to come here this evening. We'll consider the fresh facts in a moment. But before I come on to them, I want to go back to our last meeting. On that occasion I asked you a number of questions. Would either or both of you care to amend any of the answers you gave to them?'

He watched John Bayley go rigid, and jerk up his head.

'I've no idea what you can mean. The question you've just asked strikes me as highly offensive.'

Pollard turned to Lorna Bayley. Beautifully turned out, she

151

was sitting erect with hands tightly clasped, her face expression-less.

'I've nothing to add to what my husband has just said,' she replied, 'particularly about your last question being offensive.'

Without comment Pollard pressed a bell on his desk. The door opened.

'Mr James Bayley, sir,' Toye announced.

There was an electric silence. James Bayley, still unkempt, stood rooted to the spot, staring fixedly at his brother-in-law in dress suit and black tie. Finally Toye touched him on the shoulder, and he subsided mechanically on to a chair.

'You all seem to have very little to say to each other,' Pollard remarked, 'so I will do the talking. You now realize, of course, that the exchange of identity between Mr John and Mr James Bayley for the period of the *Penelope* cruise and its purpose is known to us. Mr James Bayley has, in fact, freely admitted it.'

John Bayley turned on James with an expression of such malevolence that Toye quietly took up a stance between them.

One actor, Pollard thought, in an irrelevant flash sparked off by a certain facial resemblance, but playing two characters who are worlds apart. . . .

'The purpose of the exchange is quite obvious,' he went on. 'Mrs Bayley had been left the house at Roccombe. It occupied a site next to a supermarket, the owners of which were anxious to acquire the site for purposes of expansion. Mrs Bayley was equally anxious for the deal to go through, but some local pre-servation enthusiasts succeeded in getting the house listed as of architectural and historic interest. So demolition was off, and the supermarket proprietors no longer concerned to make a deal. No doubt it was at this point that the idea of arson occurred to either Mrs Bayley or her husband. In due course Mr James Bayley was approached, and agreed—no doubt for a handsome consideration—to impersonate his brother-in-law on the recent cruise by the *Penelope* in the Mediterranean. There is, of course, a family resemblance between the two Mr Bayleys, who are cousins as well as brothers-in-law, and on the strength of this a temporary exchange of passports was risked, and proved successful.'

Pollard paused. Both the John Bayleys were staring at James, John with hatred and fury, Lorna with agonized appeal.

'To continue,' he said, 'in the course of the cruise Mr John

Bayley came back to London as his cousin James. On Thursday, April 26th, he travelled to Roccombe by train, stayed at the Railway Hotel as Mr J. Brockenhurst of Huddersfield, and that night set fire to his wife's house. He is not an arson expert, and in any case the forensic experts would have detected that the fire was started deliberately. But he might very well have made a successful getaway if there hadn't been a second person in the house that night, an elderly man whose body was found in the ruins by the fire brigade the next day.'

'You blasted fool!' John Bayley spat at James. 'Too bloody incompetent even to keep your mouth shut. All right'—he swung round to Pollard—'I fired the place, and why the hell not? It was my wife's property, and if she wanted the site cleared, she'd got a right to it. Call this a free country! It might be a communist state. I tell you, people have had about enough of this bloody interference. They won't stand for it much longer.'

'One thing that people aren't prepared to stand for, Mr Bayley,' Pollard said quietly, 'is murder. We know, you see, that the man whose body was found in the wreckage of your wife's house didn't die in the fire, his presence having been overlooked by you. His skull had been deliberately smashed in by——'

Before Toye could stop him James Bayley hurled himself at his cousin.

'You murdering devil!' he yelled. 'Dragging Lorna into this!'

The door burst open in answer to Pollard's ring, and a constable helped Toye and Longman drag the two men apart. Pollard, standing behind his desk, surveyed the scene, aware that this was the crunch.

'Of course, it's perfectly clear, Mr and Mrs Bayley,' he said, 'why you felt it was too big a risk to let Mrs Audrey Vickers go on living. She had your London address, and proposed to call. You were only safe so long as the exchange of identity by Mr John and Mr James Bayley remained undiscovered, weren't you?'

The room was very quiet. James Bayley, still breathing fast from the scuffle, stared at Pollard in blank incomprehension.

Suddenly his sister sprang to her feet, and pointed at him with a shaking hand.

'I tell you, James knows nothing about the Vickers woman,' she shouted. 'Nothing! Nothing! How could he? He'd gone from Venice before John met me, and told me he'd killed that man at Roccombe. That's when I saw that Vickers——'

Her voice cracked ominously.

After supper one evening, some weeks later, Pollard rose from his chair with a groan to answer the telephone.

'Strode here,' a voice said. 'It's honours easy: we had a daughter this afternoon. Eight pounds two ounces.'

'Terrific,' Pollard replied. 'Both doing fine, I hope?'

'Both positively bouncing. I've just come away from the hospital. They chuck you out at eight-thirty. My mother's here, holding the fort. We were wondering if you'd both care to come round tomorrow, after supper. She's just seen in the evening paper that James Bayley's been granted bail on his second application.'

'Hang on a minute,' Pollard said. 'I'll just find out from Jane how we're fixed.'

He returned to say that unless he were suddenly yanked off to a case, they would love to come.

'I agree that it was very wrong of James Bayley to go in on the arson plan,' Olivia Strode said, 'but all the same, I liked the man. I've never believed for a moment that he had anything to do with Audrey Vickers' death.'

'Your feminine intuition was absolutely sound,' Pollard replied. 'But we had to have the facts. I've been out to Italy again, you know.'

'Not again?' she exclaimed.

'I've been green with envy,' Jane Pollard remarked. 'Look how business wives gallivant all over the world, with all expenses paid.'

'Why not join Women's Lib?' suggested David Strode. 'Better still, let's park our offspring on doting grandparents, and go on an uncluttered holiday ourselves.'

'I'm on,' said Pollard. 'Reverting to James Bayley, I went out to check up on his own statement and his sister's about his movements before and after the cruise. Their statements agreed, incidentally. She's been desperately anxious to convince us that James knew nothing about either of the murders. Her concern for him's something in her favour, anyway.'

'I suppose the arson was planned some time ago?' Olivia asked.

'Yes, last summer. As soon as a preservation order was put on the house, and the deal with the supermarket people was off. James turned up at Trafalgar Terrace in October. By this time the John Bayleys were agreed that he couldn't possibly play the lead in the affair, but should be able to manage a supporting role. He was perfectly willing to come in, and admits that he saw it as a good joke. His knowledge of Venice came in very useful, of course, when the three of them got down to detailed planning.'

'The details are what I'm longing to hear about,' Olivia said. 'It seems to me that they took the most incredible risks.'

'It's amazing what you can carry off, given the nerve,' remarked her son. 'Carry on, Super.'

'It's a bit involved,' Pollard replied, 'but I'll try to be coherent. On the day the cruise started, James arrived in Venice by an early train, and left a suicase containing his personal belongings in a luggage locker at the station. Meanwhile the John Bayleys flew out to Venice from London on a morning scheduled flight, instead of coming with the bulk of the cruise passengers in the chartered planes which arrived after lunch. They had booked their return flight on the afternoon of Monday 30 April.'

'I see,' Olivia said. 'I remember Charles Moreton-Blake remarking that they'd been very lucky to get seats at such short notice.'

'Nothing foreseeable was left to chance. Later on in the morning John and James met casually, and under cover of chatting for a few minutes they exchanged passports. They are roughly the same height and colouring, and sufficiently alike to get by on the average passport scrutiny. James then joined up with his sister at a prearranged spot, and they proceeded to while away the time until embarkation as husband and wife sightseeing in Venice. John took the next train to Milan, and returned to England on James's passport, as James.'

'I suppose the Odyssey people sent prospective passenger lists to everybody who'd booked?' David Strode enquired. 'The Bayleys would have vetted theirs carefully, and just had to trust to luck that no one they knew would turn up at the last minute on a cancellation.'

'This was one of the main hazards, but their luck held. So did John's—as James—in London. No one seems to have taken any interest in him. The John Bayleys haven't been long in their present house, and James had only visited them there twice.

John stayed indoors a lot, and spent most of his time in the studio to be in character. We know that he donned hornrims for the trip to Roccombe, and probably stuck rubber pads in his cheeks, and tried a few other minor dodges to disguise himself not too obviously.

'Well, we now come to the morning of Monday, 30 April, when the *Penelope* docked at Venice. You come in here, Mrs Strode. The two Bayleys were at breakfast as usual, I imagine?'

'Yes, they certainly were,' Olivia replied. 'We were all rather early that morning, and talked about how we were going to spend the day. I can remember Mrs Bayley saying that they were going to ring their solicitor, and find out if there was really any need for them to cut short their holiday because of the fire. Immediately after breakfast I went off for the whole day with my friends. At dinner that evening the other people at our table said that the Bayleys' solicitor had strongly advised them to return at once, and they'd left on an afternoon plane.'

'In actual fact, they didn't call their solicitor. They went to an hotel and collected an envelope addressed to J. Bayley, Esq., James presenting John's passport as evidence of identity, and Mrs Bayley booking a table for lunch for two. Inside the envelope was James's passport, left there earlier by John, who had come out on a night flight. All right?'

Olivia clutched her head.

'Yes,' she said. 'But where was John Bayley in the meantime?'

Pollard grinned.

'Sunbathing on the Lido,' he said.

'Sunbathing on the Lido?' chorused his hearers incredulously.

'Why not? What can be more anonymous than a row of seminude torsos on a beach?'

'I call that a master stroke,' said David. 'Do go on. I can't wait.'

'Having now got his own passport, James returned John's to his sister, to be handed over to its owner in due course. They then went back to the *Penelope*, announced that they had to leave at once for England, and shifted their luggage by water-taxi to the air terminal. They then mingled with the crowds and parted unobtrusively. In the meantime John was organizing his return from the Lido. He either had to come by vaporetto, and risk running into cruise passengers whom he wouldn't be able to recognize, or hire a water-taxi, with a much greater risk of being

156

remembered by the boatman if questions were ever asked. He chose the water-taxi.'

'From your tone, obviously, a mistake,' Jane commented. 'But the other might have been complete disaster, too. One couldn't know.'

'No, one couldn't,' agreed her husband. 'Well, John Bayley joined up with his wife, again at some prearranged spot. One has to remember how inconspicuous meetings and partings can be in big holiday crowds like those in Venice at this time of year. She handed over his passport, and they went along to the hotel where she had booked a table for lunch. It can't have been a very successful meal. In the course of it, she learnt that her husband had killed a man at Roccombe, and he learnt from her that Audrey Vickers could turn up at any time in London and discover about the impersonation.'

'And James?' asked Olivia.

'On parting from his sister James went to the railway station, to retrieve his suitcase, and get a train out of Venice. He found that one was shortly leaving for Padua, and took a ticket. Then a hitch occurred for which he'll be thankful for the rest of his life, I should think. When he went to his luggage locker the key jammed, and he had to get help from an official. You can imagine the excitement, and the witnesses of his last-minute dash for the train.'

David Strode whistled.

'Meaning that there were witnesses to the time he left Venice, and, harking back, also a witness to the time John Bayley disembarked from his water-taxi?'

'This is it. The gist of it is that James was out of Venice half-an-hour before John returned to it from the Lido. It was the disclosures over the lunch-table which sparked off the plan to liquidate Audrey Vickers, and by that time James had vanished into the unknown. I was able to establish all this by going out to Venice: hence the success of his second application for bail.'

'I'm so thankful he's clear as far as the murder goes,' Olivia said with feeling. 'Of course, he's got a terrible time ahead of him, over his sister, I mean. His own prison sentence—I suppose he'll get one in connection with the arson conspiracy—looks like being the least part of his troubles, poor man.'

'He'll get over it all in the long term,' Pollard said with conviction. 'He's the buoyant type.'

David Strode raised his glass.

'Had I a hat,' he said, 'I'd take it off to you, Pollard.'

'Nice of you,' Pollard replied, reciprocating, 'but it's been anything but a one-man job, you know. It was Mrs Strode who put us on to the identity swop. Actually, if I'd been a bit more receptive, I should have realized that my sergeant was groping along the same line at an earlier stage in the case. It was when we were assuming that James had done the arson job. He made a remark to the effect that the artistic temperament and carefully planned arson didn't seem to hang together.'

'Is that Sergeant Toye?' Olivia asked. 'I remember him at Affacombe. Very quiet and serious, and taking it all in.'

'The same chap. Only he's just been promoted to Inspector on the strength of what he's pulled off during this Vickers affair.'

'Rather sad from your point of view, isn't it? I suppose he won't be working with you any more?'

'Indeed he will,' Pollard assured her. 'The old firm's continuing as before.'

Denise Robins

The very best and most sparkling romances
from the pen of one of our most popular
and bestselling women writers – all
available from Mayflower:

THE FLAME AND THE FROST   30p
BRIDE OF DOOM   30p
MY LADY DESTINY   30p
DANCE IN THE DUST   25p
GOLD FOR THE GAY MASTERS   30p
THE SIN WAS MINE   25p
TIME RUNS OUT   25p